The Prone Gunman

Jean-Patrick Manchette

Translated from the French by James Brook

CITY LIGHTS BOOKS
SAN FRANCISCO

10 9 8 7 6 5 4 3 2 1

Cover design and photo: Stefan Gutermuth/double-u-gee
Book design and typography: Small World Productions
The translator is deeply grateful to Donald Nicholson-Smith for his expert assistance.

This work, published as part of the program of aid for publication, received support from the French Ministry of Foreign Affairs and the Cultural Service of the French Embassy in the United States. Cet ouvrage publié dans le cadre du programme d'aide à la publication bénéficie du soutien du Ministère des Affaires Etrangères et du Service Culturel de l'Ambassade de France représenté aux Etats-Unis.

Library of Congress Cataloging-in-Publication Data

Manchette, Jean-Patrick, 1942-
[Position du tireur couché. English]
The prone gunman / by Jean-Patrick Manchette ; translated from the French by James Brook.
p. cm.
ISBN 0-87286-402-2
I. Brook, James. II. Title.
PQ2673.A452 P6713 2002
843'.914—dc21

2002024185

CITY LIGHTS BOOKS are edited by Lawrence Ferlinghetti and Nancy J. Peters and published at the City Lights Bookstore, 261 Columbus Avenue, San Francisco, CA 94133. Visit us on the Web at www.citylights.com.

1

It was winter, and it was dark. Coming down directly from the Arctic, a freezing wind rushed into the Irish Sea, swept through Liverpool, raced across the Cheshire plain (where the cats lowered their trembling ears at the sound of the roaring in the chimneys) and, through the lowered window, struck the eyes of the man sitting in the little Bedford van. The man did not blink.

He was tall but not really massive, with a calm face, blue eyes, and brown hair that just covered the tops of his ears. He wore a reefer, a black sweater, and blue jeans; he had fake Clarks on his feet. He kept his upper body erect, leaning against the right door of the cab, his legs on the bench seat, the soles touching the left door. One would have taken him for thirty or a little more; he was not quite that old. His name was Martin Terrier. An Ortgies automatic pistol with a Redfield silencer rested on his lap.

The Bedford was parked in the northern suburb of Worcester, in a residential neighborhood full of Tudor-style houses, with half-timbering and small-paned windows whose cross pieces were painted a shiny black. The gray or pastel light of television glowed behind the windows of houses without shutters. Two couples waited at the nearby bus stop, their heads bent, their backs to the wind.

A porch light came on beneath the awning of a Tudor house fifty meters from the Bedford. When the door of the house opened, Terrier tossed his French cigarette, a Gauloise, on the floorboard of the cab. He picked up the Ortgies and cocked it, while at the top of the steps Marshal Dubofsky turned to give his wife a brief kiss on the cheek. A green double-decker bus, all lit up, was approaching from the north. Crammed into a beltless putty raincoat, Dubofsky began to run on his short legs. With one hand clutching a fluffy green velvet Tyrolean hat to his head, he crossed the yard on the double, hurried down the sidewalk, and reached the stop three seconds ahead of the bus. Terrier made a small sound of irritation with the saliva in his mouth. Swinging his legs around, he took the wheel of the Bedford and set the safety of the automatic, which he put next to him on the left-hand side of the bench seat. Meanwhile, the two couples and Dubofsky were getting into the bus. Terrier allowed it to get a little ahead.

In the center of Worcester there is a square that is the terminus of several bus lines. As he was parking the Bedford there, Terrier saw Dubofsky go into a movie theater that was showing a double feature, a mediocre American thriller starring Charles Bronson along with a regional black-and-white British comedy with Diane Cilento. Once the bus passengers had dispersed, the square was deserted. Across from the theater, a pub devoid of all picturesqueness and looking more like a big launderette cast pools of yellow light on the sidewalk through its opaque windows. In her glass cube at the back of the lobby the theater cashier was knitting.

A fake redhead dressed in a poppy-red three-quarter-length coat of acrylic fur, wearing scarlet lipstick, too much mascara, and black plastic boots with very high heels, came out and left the theater. A red purse slung across her shoulder, she had her hands in her pockets and wore a sullen, calculating expression. Dubofsky followed twenty meters behind; he cast a furtive glance toward the pub.

When the girl and the man were away from the theater and were about to go around the corner, Terrier released the clutch and caught up with and overtook them. Just before the redhead reached the intersection, he swerved, pulled up to the sidewalk, and came to a stop. With the engine running, Terrier opened the left door and stepped out onto the sidewalk, with the Ortgies in his hand. Dubofsky almost ran into him. Their eyes met. Dubofsky opened his mouth to shout. Terrier quickly shot him once in his open mouth and again at the base of his nose.

At the discreet sound of these shots, the redhead turned. Terrier also turned, and they found themselves face to face just as Dubofsky's head, which was split open, full of holes, and shattered like the shell of a hard-boiled egg, hit the sidewalk with a squishy sound. Terrier took two steps forward, extended his arm, put the silencer against the girl's heart, and pressed the trigger once. The girl flew back, her intestines emptying noisily, and fell dead on her back. Terrier got back in the Bedford and left.

He turned left once again and drove westward down an absolutely deserted shopping street where the violent wind pursued dirty newspaper pages. Behind the dark shopwindows were hundreds of empty suits, thousands of empty shoes, thousands of square cardboard labels bearing prices in pounds sterling and occasionally in guineas.

The Bedford soon rejoined the highway. Around midnight it passed Oxford. Later it reached London.

Terrier was staying at the Cavendish Hotel. He parked the little van in the hotel lot, went up to his room, and from the individual automatic bar removed a split of Spanish champagne. He drank a glassful, then poured the rest of the sparkling wine down the toilet and tossed the bottle into a corner of the room. He opened a bottle of Watney's "strong ale" and sipped it as he reclined on the bed, his upper body erect, and smoked two or three cigarettes. He was almost motionless and did not seem sleepy. Then he got back up, dismantled the weapon, cleaned it meticulously, and put it away in a cardboard box. He smoked another cigarette, then put on his pajamas, got into bed, and turned out the light.

2

A Jamaican woman brought Terrier his breakfast on time, at eight-thirty. The man ate quickly. His features were a little haggard, his eyes looked a little tired, and the edges of his eyelids were red. He placed the tray in the hallway. He groomed himself and got dressed. He was just finishing adjusting his navy-blue knit tie over his light-blue shirt when someone gave eleven quick knocks on the door, followed by three more. Terrier slipped on the jacket of his gray suit and went to the door. A young guy came in: he was blond and fat, with sideburns; his green blazer and tie displayed the identical crest.

"Did you know who the girl was?" he asked, after closing the door.

Terrier shrugged. The young guy smelled of aftershave. He had big gray eyes. He smiled feebly.

"That's even better," he said. "The police are questioning the husband. Do you have the gun?"

With a nod, Terrier indicated the cardboard box. The young blond guy with sideburns put it under his arm.

"Till next time."

"Maybe."

The blond guy smiled. He went out, closing the door soundlessly. Terrier shrugged again. In an ashtray decorated with an advertisement for something called "Younger's Tartan," which was probably a beer, he burned the photograph of Dubofsky that was still in his possession. He threw the ashes in the toilet and then went downstairs with his baggage, which he checked with the hotel. He paid his bill, took the little Bedford van from the parking lot, and went to return it to the garage where he had rented it, in Camden, in North London. It was cold and dry. Still windy. Terrier took the bus back toward the center of town, to Soho. He bought a few things and walked around. Greek Street was full of Chinese. In a dusty shop an old man offered Terrier a pirated Maria Callas recording, but Terrier already had it.

In the middle of the afternoon, he returned on foot to the Cavendish Hotel and claimed his baggage. A taxi took him to the airport. A lot of police officers and soldiers were stationed at the entrance to check vehicles and people because of a recent resurgence of Irish terrorism.

The airplane took off twenty minutes late and touched down early in the evening at Roissy–Charles de Gaulle. Around nine-thirty, a French taxi dropped Terrier in front of his building on Boulevard Lefebvre, across from the Parc des Expositions, not far from the Porte de Versailles.

Terrier went up on foot. There was no elevator. The man's apartment was a studio under the mansard roof, on the top floor. The telephone was ringing inside when Terrier reached his landing. As Terrier opened the door and entered, the telephone stopped ringing. The man closed the door behind him, turned on the light, and stood still for a moment, his traveling bag set on the floor nearby.

The single room, flanked by a kitchenette and a toilet and shower, was sparsely furnished. A white bed, a beige shag carpet, two white plastic-covered armchairs, a coffee table—that was just about it. A large, spherical Chinese lantern made of white paper hung from the ceiling, and, by way of a bedside lamp, a black steel spotlight was attached to the wall near the bed with an X hook. Against the back wall, paperback books and records were piled on the floor. A bearded black man in a buff suit and a canary-yellow turtleneck shirt was sitting in one of the white armchairs.

"It's me," he said.

"You scared me," said Terrier.

"Sorry."

Terrier picked up his bag and advanced into the studio.

"How did you get in?"

"Are you joking, Christian?" asked the black man.

Terrier put his bag down under a window. He went over to the kitchenette and put ice into a wine glass, poured vodka over it, and added a few drops of lemon juice. He served himself a bottle of overchilled Mutzig beer. He came back into the room and handed the wine glass of vodka to the black man, who had remained seated but had stretched out his legs. He wore black cotton socks and very soft leather shoes.

"Well?" asked Terrier.

"There are rumors going around. Are you getting out, Christian?"

"Who's saying that?"

"Cox."

"He told you that?"

"He told someone. He's very worried."

"Did he send you?"

The black man shook his head without smiling.

"Cox is a nutcase, a worm, and a faggot," he said. "I came to wait for you because I wanted to make sure that no one else was waiting for you."

"Why?"

"I was the one who recruited you."

"So?"

The black man shook his head with an absent look.

"There were some guys fomenting guerilla war in Asia," he said. "When circumstances changed, they had to drop everything. Some took it badly. Some are still in psychoanalysis. Some became Buddhists. You understand? That far gone." He took a swallow of his lemon-flavored vodka. "I'm not nearly that far gone. All the same, I was the one who recruited you."

The telephone rang. Terrier answered. Cox was at the other end of the line.

"I've just gotten back," said Terrier. "It went well."

"Yes. This time, I'll pay you in person."

"Fine," said Terrier. He frowned a little.

"Rue de Varenne," said Cox. "Tomorrow morning, at nine."

"Fine," said Terrier again.

He hung up and glanced at the black man, who was resting the ends of his index fingers against his nostrils and rocking slightly in the armchair. Terrier picked up the receiver again but didn't bring it to his ear.

"See you later."

The black man picked up a black suitcase and went toward the door.

"Cox will first try to convince you," he said. "Don't burn your bridges. If you get in a jam, you know where to reach me."

"Yes."

"I'm not staying for dinner," declared the black man as he opened the door. "You won't tell me what you're thinking. You're suspicious of me. I'm offended, Christian."

"So long," said Martin Terrier. The black man left, closing the door behind him. Terrier dialed a number as he listened to the black man's steps recede on the stairs. He heard the ringing on the other end of the line, which went on for a long time till Alex answered.

"Oh! You're back," she shouted happily and breathlessly. "I was afraid you wouldn't come back till tomorrow. In fact, I was on the stairs—I was going to the movies. Are you coming over?"

"No. I haven't eaten. Come over when you get out of the movies."

"You're crazy. I'll come over right now!"

"No," said Terrier again. "I have to have dinner with someone."

"A lady or a gentleman?"

"A guy. Come around twelve-thirty."

"Oh." Alex sounded disappointed. "Should I bring Sudan?" she asked.

"Please."

"I love you. I missed you."

"Yes, me too. See you soon."

They hung up. Terrier slowly drank his beer, standing up, frowning. Then he quickly went to the kitchenette to put his glass in the sink and to open a cupboard that contained a few dishes and a wooden box. He took down the box, which contained a Heckler & Koch HK4 automatic pistol with interchangeable barrels. He checked the cleanliness of the various parts of the gun, then assembled it with a .32 ACP barrel and the appropriate magazine. He went and put the automatic under the pillow on his bed, then went back to the kitchenette, where he drank another beer and, standing up, ate a can of beans and sausage and a piece of Gruyère.

By the time Alex let herself in with her key, Terrier had long since finished tidying up. Sitting in an armchair, he was reading a science-fiction novel and listening to Radio Luxembourg on a small receiver.

Alex was a twenty-seven-year-old brunette with short hair,

striking blue eyes, high cheekbones, and a beautifully formed neck and jaw line. She was tall with long legs and breasts almost as firm as her thighs. She was dressed now in a three-piece light-gray pantsuit and a white shirt. She had a white leather handbag on her shoulder and in her hand a rectangular wicker basket with a top. Sudan meowed in the basket. Alex kissed Terrier, who returned her kiss.

"Your movie was all right?"

"It was shitty. I left before the end, and I had a drink while waiting to come over. Dinner was okay?"

Terrier shrugged. He took the basket, put it down on the floor, and opened it. Sudan got his footing and began roaming around the studio, sniffing and coolly looking things over. Finally, he went into the kitchenette and began eating from the bowl that Terrier had filled for him. Meanwhile, Alex had gone over to the coffee table, on which stood gift-wrapped boxes.

"You're nice," she said.

"They're to say goodbye," said Terrier.

"Excuse me?"

"It has nothing to do with you. It has nothing to do with anything. I told you that one day I would have to leave suddenly—and alone. You remember. Well, this is it."

With a calm and dreamy look, Alex pushed the boxes to the end of the table. It took her three matches to light her Benson & Hedges.

"You've found something better?" she asked.

"Not at all," said Terrier. "Not at all. There's no other woman."

Between clenched teeth, Alex uttered an obscene curse. Terrier looked at her silently, then went into the kitchenette to fill a glass with vodka. When he returned, Alex was bent over the books piled against the wall and stuffing volumes under her arm.

"This one's mine," she was saying. "And this. And this. And this." She turned around without standing up straight and winked at Terrier. "Okay," she said. "As we agreed. No questions. No dramatics. Okay."

"Fine," said Terrier. "You can have all the books. I'm not taking them."

He went and turned off the radio. Alex, the books in her arms, came back to the coffee table. She was stumbling a little. She tapped the rim of her glass against her teeth as she drained it. The ice cubes tinkled. In her hurry, she had wet her upper lip and the bottom of her nose.

"I'll call you a taxi," said Terrier. "Don't forget your presents."

Alex burst out laughing. She dropped her glass, which didn't break against the carpet. She ran to the kitchenette, dug in a drawer, and came back with a carving knife. With the handle against her belly, she held the blade straight in front of her. Her teeth were bared, and her makeup was running.

"Stop," said Terrier, without moving.

"Fucking asshole."

She took a step forward. Terrier put his weight on his left leg and held the outstretched fingers of his right hand tightly together, his arm slightly bent. But the young woman shook her head violently and contented herself with throwing the knife at the window. It knocked against the glass and fell to the floor. Alex shook her head again.

"You're taking Sudan into your new life?"

"Yes."

"He won't like that."

"Yes, he will."

"Christian," said Alex, "let me have the poor cat. As a souvenir. Please." She seemed unaware that tears were now streaking her face; she was smiling.

"You're being stupid."

Alex nodded. Terrier picked up the phone and called a taxi. There would be a five-minute wait. He remained standing. Alex got her things and her presents together.

"Sudan won't be happy with you," she said. "You're abnormal. You're sick in the head. I tried. God knows, I tried!"

She didn't say what she had tried. Before leaving, as she passed in front of Terrier, she raised herself on tiptoe and spit clumsily in his face.

3

The Rue de Varenne apartment was a duplex located in the rear of an old town house, on a paved courtyard, above stables that had been transformed into private garages. In the courtyard, the name "Lionel Perdrix" appeared on a framed visiting card above the doorbell. A few seconds before nine, Terrier rang the doorbell seven short times, pushed open the gate, and climbed the flight of outside stairs. The remote-control lock of the white-lacquered entryway door buzzed and clicked, and Terrier opened the door, closed it behind him, and climbed another flight of stairs, these covered in gray carpet. He emerged into the vast gray-and-white duplex full of ultramodern furniture and Pop, Op, and kinetic art.

Cox was seated on the edge of a gigantic white leather sofa, his back to a windowless wall with a balcony overhead. A short guy with black eyes, his hands in the pockets of a gray overcoat, leaned out with his belly against the balcony railing; his eyes never left Terrier.

Bent over a low, openwork white-lacquered table, Cox was eating a copious brunch of eggs, bacon, grilled sausages, thick little pancakes, and maple syrup, accompanied by black coffee.

"I didn't have time to eat this morning," he said as Terrier came in. "Nor to sleep much, either. I had to discuss your case, Christian."

His lips were sticky with syrup; he patted them with a paper napkin and glanced at Terrier with a look of embarrassment. Tall and fleshy, he had a large pink face, a small nose, and a pouty little mouth. His short dull-blond hair was impeccably trimmed. He had not taken off his camel's-hair overcoat. Beside him on the sofa lay a twisted blue-and-yellow plaid scarf. Terrier opened his brown leather coat, but he didn't take it off. He sat down across from Cox in an enormous armchair that matched the sofa.

"He's armed," said the short guy on the balcony without taking his eyes off Terrier.

Cox directed a friendly grimace at Terrier.

"Why did you kill the girl, too?" he asked.

"Is that a problem?"

"Not at all. She was his mistress. Not at all important. I'm just asking. You've never killed anyone who was not a target."

"I was in a hurry."

"I see," said Cox. "You're saying it jokingly, but it probably is the reason."

"I'm not joking," said Terrier.

Cox gulped down a bit of pancake dripping with melted butter and syrup, then shook his head with his eyelids lowered. As he ate, he leaned over and sighed and opened a leather briefcase at the foot of the sofa. Unhurriedly, he withdrew a brown package that could have been a ream of paper and pushed it across the table in Terrier's direction. Terrier weighed the package in his hands. He looked at Cox.

"There's a bonus," said Cox. Linguistic details betrayed the fact that French was not his mother tongue. But he had no trace of an accent.

"Thanks."

"There's a rumor that you're going to get out, Christian."

"A rumor? That would surprise me."

"You've sold your car, you've bought another one, you've given notice on your apartment. Various other things."

"Okay," said Martin Terrier. "I'm getting out."

"It seems that you're not going to work for someone else. You're simply going to get out. I can easily understand that. Still, you should have talked to me about it. You can't just disappear without warning."

"But that's just what I'm going to do."

"We're not in agreement," said Cox. "Obviously, no one can force you, not with the kind of work you do."

"That's what I thought." Terrier smiled.

"The company has an important project in preparation," said Cox. "Just one, as far as you're concerned. You can get out afterward. I daresay we'll even make things easier for you. You know we can make things easier. On the other hand, we can make a lot of difficulties for you."

"I'd advise against trying to fuck with me." Terrier smiled again.

"For this project you can name your price. What if we said one hundred and fifty thousand French francs?"

Terrier shook his head.

"Two hundred thousand," said Cox.

Terrier stood up, the brown package under his arm.

"Sorry. Not at any price. I'm going now."

At a nonchalant pace, he withdrew as far as the staircase, the package under his left arm, his right arm partially bent. His blue eyes darted from Cox to the short guy on the balcony.

"Too bad," said Cox. "Drive safely. If you ever want to get in contact with me, run an ad in *Le Monde* in the public announcements section. Never try to get in contact through other channels."

"Goodbye," said Terrier.

He went downstairs, crossed the paved courtyard, and left

through a covered passage and a porte cochere. He headed toward the Seine, hailed a Mercedes taxi that was going by, had himself taken to Barbès, took the metro, changed lines two or three times, and found himself back in the open air at the Notre-Dame-de-Lorette station. He had an eleven o'clock appointment with his financial adviser. He was early, so he waited at a café counter with an espresso that tasted like leather.

Faulques, the financial adviser, lived in a ground-floor apartment on Rue de la Victoire, at the back of the courtyard, in two cramped rooms, one of which functioned as an office. He sometimes left the communicating door ajar, exposing a badly made-up bed with grayish sheets in the other room. Faulques was short, ugly, and bald, and he had two blackheads and a dirty, idiotic little mustache. Winter and summer he answered the door in shirtsleeves, his striped pants held up by tight elastic suspenders that crossed in the back. He was voluble and nervous and smoked hard-as-rock Toscanellis that were always going out.

"I don't inspire confidence," he had once said to Terrier. "People mistrust me because I look seedy. Oh, yes! I look seedy, Monsieur Charles. I look like a swindler!" He was shouting, even though Terrier had not tried to contradict him. "A good financial adviser should look prosperous. That's what people think. But I don't have the time. Do you want to know why?"

"Yes," Terrier said patiently.

"Because I spend all my time taking care of money," said Faulques triumphantly. "I make it move. I like that. Nothing else interests me. Neither food nor fucking nor dressing a little better: nothing. Do you understand what it means to have only one thing on your mind?"

"Maybe."

Faulques had shaken his head skeptically and proceeded to show Terrier a photograph of his two adolescent girls, whom he saw once a month (he was divorced).

At eleven o'clock Terrier rang at Faulques's door. He handed over the brown package and gave him detailed instructions. Faulques took notes and ventured a few comments. Then Terrier left.

A light sleet had begun to fall, turning to water as it landed. Terrier took the metro back to the Opéra station and returned home in a taxi.

Reaching his landing, Terrier saw that the door to his apartment was slightly ajar. He dropped to one knee as he drew his HK4 from under his jacket. Holding the weapon in both hands and pointing it at the doorjamb, he froze. He breathed slowly through the mouth in order to hear better. He heard nothing but the distant sounds of the street and the piano on the third floor on which someone was vainly and obstinately attempting to get the first twelve measures of the supposedly *Pathetic Sonata* right.

Suddenly, Terrier jumped forward, pushed the door open with his shoulder, and tumbled into the middle of the studio apartment. As he lay on his back, and after his eyes and the barrel of his automatic had quickly swept the room in all directions, the man slowly relaxed and lowered his arms. His joined hands and his weapon came to rest on his thighs. There was no one in the apartment. The pianist on the third floor had given up, and not even the tick-tock of the alarm clock could be heard. Actually, the alarm clock was busted up. The furniture was busted up, too—the armchairs gutted, the bedding torn up, the record player demolished. Terrier's luggage had been slashed open with a knife and his things—now torn and filthy—scattered all over the studio. In the kitchenette, the cupboard doors had been pulled off and the dishes smashed.

Terrier got back up, returned the HK4 to its cloth shoulder holster, and closed the door. It had not been forced. He went into the kitchenette. On the linoleum was a filthy magma of mustard, flour, sugar, spices, liquor, broken dishes, and garbage.

"Sudan!" Terrier called softly.

He made little sounds with his mouth to entice the tomcat to come out. He frowned. He went to look under the bed, then went back to the kitchenette, swearing through his teeth.

On top of the refrigerator was a small key ring on a sheet of squared paper. Terrier examined the keys and the message on the piece of paper, which read: "I'm taking Sudan. Fuck you." Alex had even signed it.

Terrier put the keys in his pocket and shook his head. His frown vanished. He laughed silently, then shook his head again and gloomily considered the mess.

It took him almost three hours to clean up and rearrange everything. He put to one side those of his things that were intact. Everything else was put into the gutted luggage, which Terrier tied up with string and took down to the garbage along with the rest of the mess. He had to make several trips. He took advantage of one of these journeys to continue on to a nearby Prisunic, where he bought a suitcase and a bag. Back upstairs, he packed up his remaining possessions.

Then his lips tightened. He picked up the intact telephone and dialed a number. The call went through on the first ring.

"Hello, don't hang up," said Alex's voice. "You have reached Alexa Métayer. I will be out for a few hours. At the tone, please leave your name and telephone number so I can call you back when I return."

Terrier shrugged and hung up. He finished his tasks, then picked up the telephone again to call the owner, who lived on the first floor of the building. While the man was on his way upstairs, Terrier called his garage to have his car brought round.

"Oh, my," declared the owner when he saw the damage. He let out a whistle.

"I'll forget the deposit," said Terrier. "I'll leave you what remains of the furniture. That all right with you?"

"Yes, fine," said the owner after a moment's reflection. "I don't want to be mean about it. What happened?"

"A girl got worked up. You know how it is."

"The pretty brunette?" The owner made a face. "You wouldn't believe it to look at her. I saw her going out late in the morning. I don't know when she arrived, of course."

He winked at Terrier. Terrier turned his back on him. The telephone rang. Terrier lifted the receiver.

"I'm trying to reach Luigi."

The voice was slurred, metallic, abnormally shrill. The guy (or the girl) at the other end of the line was using a vocoder-like gadget to distort the sound—or else he was a rehabilitated mute.

"What number are you calling?" asked Terrier.

He was cut off. Terrier hung up. A second later, the telephone began ringing again.

"Hello?"

"I can't reach Luigi Rossi anymore," said the deformed

voice. "I'm furious. Somebody will have to pay for that. Maybe you."

"Explain that," said Terrier.

There was a noise that could have been a chuckle, then the line went dead. This time no one called back. Someone rang at the door, but it was only the guy from the garage coming to say that the Citroën DS 21 was parked out in front. Terrier pocketed the car keys and tipped the worker, who went away. A moment later, Terrier and the owner came downstairs together.

"You'll be missed," the owner was saying. "You were the ideal tenant. Peace and quiet and all. If I understand correctly" (he gave Terrier a complicitous smile), "you had some private problems."

"I wouldn't call that a problem," said Terrier.

It was five-thirty in the afternoon. Terrier tossed his luggage on the backseat of the old DS 21, grabbed the wheel, and started the engine. He took the service road toward the Porte de Versailles and then slipped into the slow and very heavy traffic. An old pale-gray Ford Capri with a dull black hood began to tail him.

4

To connect with the Autoroute du Sud, Terrier had to turn around and double back at the jammed-up Porte de Versailles. He noticed that a Ford Capri was doing the same. Through the flood of automobiles and exhaust fumes he poked along the outer boulevards to the Porte d'Orléans, then up the access ramp to the highway and along the highway itself. The Capri was still in sight.

Around six-thirty, Terrier was no more than thirty kilometers from Paris, but by then the traffic was loosening up. The Capri was still in sight, far behind. Terrier accelerated to 125 kmh, and the Capri did the same. He reduced his speed to 90 kmh. The Capri maintained its distance.

As he approached the Achères parking area, Terrier slowed down even more. He considered the failing light and the traffic. It was still light, and many vehicles were still on the road. Terrier didn't stop: he sped up and then maintained a normal speed. Now and again he glanced at the rearview mirror. Night fell.

Around ten-thirty, Terrier wasn't far from Poitiers. Noticing a sign indicating a refueling area, he braked long and slow. He slowed down in stages, and his taillights illuminated as he did so. He left the highway and stopped under the canopy of the gas station, where he had the tank filled and various things checked and the windshield cleaned.

The Capri also needed fuel. It parked under the canopy at some distance from the DS. Terrier went to the toilet to take a piss. As he came back to his car, he went by the rear of the Capri and glanced at his shadow, who had not gotten out of the car. He was a tall, thin young man with a pasty complexion. He wore a black leather jacket and dark glasses; his head bristled with a thatch of black hair. Terrier returned to the DS, paid the attendant, and got back behind the wheel. A little sleet swirled in the orange glow of the highway lighting. Terrier started the car and went and parked in the lot behind the self-service restaurant.

The restaurant interior was done up in orange and black plastic, and there was not a single diner. This was not the sort of place to linger over a meal. As Terrier was putting food on his tray, out of the corner of his eye he saw that the Capri was pulling into the lot. It stopped, and its driver did not get out.

As Terrier was eating, a Volvo parked in the lot. A rather pretty, fortyish brunette with a fine complexion got out and came into the restaurant with two children, who were kicking up a fuss. The woman scolded and cajoled them calmly, patiently, and firmly. Terrier observed her. He had an attentive, approving expression. The fussing of the two kids made his mouth tighten a little.

When he had finished eating, Terrier returned to the DS. He glanced at the Capri, parked thirty meters away, just as a cigarette flared red. He grabbed the suitcase from the backseat, opened it on the front seat, and removed the box into which he had put the HK4 before leaving. He fitted a .380 ACP barrel into the lock, then loaded and inserted a clip. He put the automatic in the side pocket of his leather coat and got back out of his car. It was cold. What looked like snowdrifts lined the edges of the parking area. The orange lamps gave little light. In the Capri, the pale young man smoked an American cigarette. He gave Terrier a panicky look as he approached.

"Why are you following me?"

"What did you say?"

Through the open window, Terrier hit the young man between the eyes with the barrel of the HK4. The cigarette fell. Dazed, the young man sucked air through his thin mouth, his face contorted. Terrier opened the door, grabbed the young man by the front of his white sweater, and yanked him from his seat. He laid him out on the ground. The young man tried to get back up. Terrier kicked him in the head, and the young man stopped moving. Terrier quickly searched him. In ten or fifteen minutes, the pretty mom and her brats would come back this way and turn on their headlights.

In his pockets, the pallid fellow had a Swiss Army knife, keys, a plastic coin-purse, a pack of Winstons, a Bic lighter, and a wallet of the kind Africans sell on the street. In the wallet, Terrier found five hundred francs in new one-hundred-franc bills held together with a pin, along with three worn ten-franc bills; some Mobil gas coupons; an identity card, a social security card, automobile registration papers, and a certificate of insurance in the name of Alfred Chaton, packer, living in Montreuil; and a love letter from a girl. The man called Alfred Chaton began to move. Terrier pinched his temples to accelerate his coming-to, then he grabbed him, knocked his head against the car body, and, holding him by the hair, raked his face against the handle of the back door. Finally, he sat him on the ground, leaned him up against the Capri, and slapped him.

"Christ stop you're crazy," Alfred moaned. "I don't know anything. I'm just a gofer."

"Why are you following me?"

"They asked me to."

"They who?"

"Some people."

Terrier gave him a kick in the spleen. Alfred convulsed and fell on his side, writhing about and groaning loudly. Terrier grasped his nose between thumb and index finger, forcing him to breathe through his mouth and preventing him from crying out as the brunette and her two kids got back into their Volvo, fifty meters away, and drove off.

"They who?" repeated Terrier. "Want me to start over?"

"Please, no. Some people. Some people called Rossi. Italians."

Suddenly, Terrier remembered the name. And he remembered Luigi Rossi appearing on a motorcycle on the twists and turns of the road that connects Albenga with Garessio in northern Italy. Remembered wearing Polaroid glasses as he stretched out between the rocks in a blind made of fir-tree branches. Remembered removing the snow protector from the barrel of his Vostok and aiming at the motorcyclist, holding his breath, and pressing the trigger. Remembered how Luigi Rossi fell on the wet road and tried to get back up; remembered how the second 7.62mm bullet hit his forehead, and pieces of helmet and head flew about. Remembered how Luigi Rossi fell back face down on the wet road, assuredly dead, and how he, Terrier, quickly returned to his Peugeot 403, which was equipped with chains, on the forest road and went back to Turin.

He remembered. At the time, he was a beginner. Cox paid him twenty thousand francs.

"Do these people called Rossi have first names?"

"They didn't say."

"They just told you that they were called Rossi," suggested Terrier.

"Yes. Well, no. I heard them talking among themselves.

They are brothers or cousins or something. I don't know."

"They are brothers or cousins or something, and they don't call each other by the first name—they call each by the family name?"

"I don't know. Yes."

"I think you could describe them for me," said Terrier.

"Absolutely," said the pale young man.

"Get back in your heap."

Grimacing with pain and fear, Alfred Chaton heaved himself into the Capri.

"What are you going to do with me? I'm just a gofer, for God's sake. I will tell you anything you want to know."

"Was it you who ransacked my apartment?"

"What? No. No."

"Do you know who did?"

"Absolutely not."

With his left hand, Terrier grabbed him by the collar and pushed him back into the Capri. At the same time, he got behind the wheel, took out his automatic, and rested the end of the barrel against the pale young man's throat.

"Don't make the slightest move, no matter what."

The young man blinked. Terrier pressed the cigarette lighter. The eyes of the motionless young man followed his gestures.

"I'm going to burn out an eye," said Terrier.

"Why? Why? You're crazy!"

The young man began to weep. With a click, the cigarette lighter popped out, ready for use.

"They told me to tell you that!" the young man cried out. "They told me to follow you and that you would spot me and to say that I was paid by some people called Rossi! I swear, it's the truth!"

"Who?"

"I don't know. I don't know them. I can describe them."

"Don't bother."

"The fucking cunts!" cried the pale young man. "They said you were an okay guy, that you might knock me around a little, but I only had to say I was a gofer and give you the name of the Rossi brothers and you would let me go! You're going to let me go now, aren't you?"

"Sure."

Terrier drew back a little on his seat and stopped pressing the barrel of the HK4 against the throat of the young man. The latter tearfully rubbed his neck.

"Oh! Thank you, thank you!"

"Take this message to Cox," said Terrier as he put a slug into his heart.

5

Terrier stopped at a motel around midnight, eighty kilometers from the place where he had killed the pale young man. At the reception desk, a false blonde with delicate features, wearing a heavy, ribbed navy-blue sweater and flannel pants, was reading beneath a desk lamp. She had awe-inspiring breasts and eyelashes. Terrier took her for about twenty-six. She gave him a key.

"What are you reading?" he asked.

Silently, she showed him the cover of her book.

"It's a story about time travel," she said. "Does that make you laugh? You think it's childish?"

"Not in the least. I'm all for time travel," said Terrier. "Besides, that's exactly what I'm doing."

The girl gave him a tired, hostile look.

"You're trying to get me interested?"

"Not really," said Terrier. "Good night."

He found his room, washed his face, put on his pajamas, picked up the telephone, and asked for Alex's number. It was one o'clock in the morning. It served her right if he woke her up. But he got the answering machine again. He waited for the beep. He had nothing to say to Alex.

"You can keep the cat, you idiot," he said.

It began snowing during the night. It was still dark and still snowing when Terrier left the motel. Just after, he left the highway and headed west. The bad weather slowed him down. It was almost noon when the DS reached Nauzac. It wasn't snowing there.

Terrier drove slowly all through the town. At one end of the town, a small, low, white perfume factory had recently been built. In the center of town, traffic was heavy and slow. Several times, Terrier almost headed the wrong way down one-way streets. There were parking meters in the neighborhood of the subprefecture, most of them adorned with stickers that read "NO! No parking meters in Nauzac!" and gave the address of the residents' action committee.

Eventually, the DS left the center of town and plunged into the residential neighborhood, where it drew up near a posh little apartment house. Leaving the engine running, Terrier got out on the sidewalk side. He remained motionless for a second. He seemed to hesitate. He blinked slowly several times. Then he strode to the entrance of the building and examined the mailboxes in the hallway. A West Indian concierge came out of her lodge. Terrier turned away.

"Are you looking for something?"

He turned to the concierge, shook his head, and then nodded.

"Mademoiselle Freux."

The woman looked perplexed, then raised her chin.

"Monsieur and Madame Freux passed away," she said.

"I didn't know. And their daughter?"

"Madame Schrader?" asked the concierge. "Madame Schrader?" she repeated impatiently, since Terrier did not reply.

"Yes," Terrier said at last. A thin white line had appeared around his mouth.

"She doesn't live very far from here. Let me get you the exact address."

She went back inside her lodge, leaving the glass door open. Terrier turned on his heel. By the time the West Indian woman came out with a piece of paper in her hand, he was already back in the DS and on his way.

He had lunch in the center. The exterior of the Brasserie des Fleurs dated from the nineteenth century and had recently been restored. The interior was full of leather-trimmed booths, little wooden partitions, and decorated frosted-glass panels as well as various modern additions. There were few customers. Terrier sat down in a booth. A bleary-eyed sexagenarian waiter, in a long apron and black jacket, came to take his order. Terrier stared at him as he ordered andouillettes and Munich beer. The waiter noted the order and went away. When he returned with the food and the glass of beer, Terrier tapped his elbow with three fingers.

"Can't quite place me, Dédé?"

The waiter looked at him with suspicion, then sucked air. His red eyes filled with tears.

"God in heaven!" he whispered.

Terrier invited him to sit down. Dédé glanced furtively toward the kitchen and the register and said that he couldn't.

"I have to attend to the room," he explained. "Martin Terrier! Well, in the name of God, shit!" He rubbed his eyes and forehead with the rag he used to wipe tables. "You've become a real gentleman. If only your father could see you!"

"That would only irritate him," said Terrier.

"You're in business?"

"That's right."

"You've come back to see this damn town. You've come back to piss on them all."

"Not especially," said Terrier.

Dédé nodded his head and smiled nastily. He was looking off into space and no longer at Terrier, who was attacking his rubbery andouillette.

"You shouldn't stay, you know," whispered Dédé.

"Excuse me?"

"This is a rotten place to be. Your father and I could have done great things if we'd only remained in Paris. You shouldn't live here."

"Okay."

"Dédé!" yelled a sort of manager, a short rat-faced man whose mustache had all of three hairs, from the direction of the register.

Dédé groaned, nodded for Terrier's benefit, and went off, dragging his feet. Terrier made himself eat half of what he'd been served, passed up both dessert and coffee, left the full amount of the check on the table along with a big tip, and walked out of the brasserie without seeing Dédé again.

Back in the DS, he consulted the Michelin guide. Nauzac boasted some half-dozen low-quality hotels and two more ambitious, if timeworn, establishments. One of them merited the pictogram that signifies "quiet" while the other was awarded the same pictogram in red, which signifies "very quiet." Terrier started off in the direction of the second hotel.

At the far end of a small French-style garden, the hotel was a big limestone building with a slate roof, with many turrets and big wooden shutters with paint flaking off. The driveway between the gravel paths was muddy. On the central lawn, an empty Kronenbourg bottle lay next to a ceramic imp, and the effluvium of hot cooking fat was in the air. Things were a little better inside, though dusty. There were many carpets, wall hangings, varnished wood, a young clerk in a burgundy jacket, and, acting as the bellboy, an immaculate chambermaid to whom Terrier turned over his travel bag. They reached the third and last floor by means of a very narrow elevator, evidently a more recent addition. The room was vast, with a high ceiling, moldings, a very big bed, and antique furniture. There were rust tracks in the bathtub, but it was grand, enormous. No bar. Terrier had a bottle of J&B, ice, and a six-pack of ginger ale sent up, along with a telephone directory for the département. He poured himself a glass, picked up the telephone, and called Anne.

"Anne Schrader speaking. Hello."

"It's Martin," said Terrier.

"Hello? What number are you calling?"

"Anne, it's Martin Terrier. I'm in town."

"You've misdialed," said the neutral voice, and Anne hung up.

Terrier gave a small sigh. After an instant of immobility, he consulted the yellow pages and found the number of the Freux Electrical Company. (In point of fact, it was a small factory utilizing exclusively female manual labor to assemble record players based on turntables manufactured elsewhere.) He called and asked for Félix Schrader. He was asked who was calling. He gave his name. Félix was put on the line.

"Well, what do you know!" exclaimed Félix Schrader. "Martin Terrier! Is it really you? Where are you?" His voice slipped out of control. He tried for baritone but slid toward countertenor at the end of each of his exclamations.

"In town. I've come back."

"You're back? For good?"

"I don't know yet."

"Great!" Félix seemed truly happy. "We'll have a drink? Wait!" Terrier waited. "Would you like to come eat at home?" asked Félix after a moment.

"I wouldn't want to impose."

Félix said not at all, not at all, he had to come, that very evening.

"Say," he asked, "did you know that I married Anne Freux?"

"I heard. Congratulations."

"Thanks. I'll give you the address. Eight o'clock this evening, okay?"

Terrier said it was okay and took down the address. He lay down on the bed, his glass within reach, his hands under his neck. Later, he suddenly awoke bathed in sweat, with a coated tongue. It was dark outside the window and in the room. He turned on the lights. In the mirror of the armoire his yellow reflection looked back with suspicion. It was exactly seven in the evening.

Because of the damage done his wardrobe during the ransacking of his apartment, Terrier didn't have much choice in what to wear. He went into the bathroom with a powder-blue suit, a blue shirt, and a tie with blue stripes. He showered, shaved, and changed. No matter how hard he brushed his teeth, he couldn't get rid of the metallic taste in his mouth.

The hotel lobby was brilliantly illuminated when Terrier came downstairs, and people were heading toward the bar and chattering. There were two or three affluent couples and a group of loudmouthed males. Everyone was obviously over forty-five and pretty well heeled.

A counter sold newspapers, cigarettes, and trinkets. Terrier bought Gauloises and glanced at the newspapers. A bad photograph of Alex was on the front page of *France-Soir.* Terrier bought the newspaper and got into his car, which was parked in the driveway. He checked his watch and turned on the overhead light to read what they were saying about Alex.

She had been killed between midnight and three in the morning, after being raped and tortured at length. It was the cleaning lady who had discovered the corpse in the morning. According to her neighbors, the young woman led a very free life. According to investigators, there were at least three aggressors. The police claimed to have a solid lead.

As he read, Terrier brought his thumb and index finger to his face and mechanically smoothed his eyebrows. Then he threw the newspaper on the floor of the DS, turned off the overhead light, and passed the palm of his hand across his forehead to smooth it out. He seemed to reflect for a moment. He did not seem shocked. Perhaps he experienced a little sadness. Certainly he must have been thinking, for his face was screwed up in concentration.

After a moment, he clicked his tongue and started the engine. He continued to frown all the way to his destination.

The Schraders' house was a sort of elegant wooden chalet painted white and bright blue, with a well-kept yard, in the middle of a neighborhood of analogous residences. It had a wooden awning over the front door, and under the awning was an electric lamp that lit up as soon as Terrier rang the doorbell. And so, when the door swung open on Anne, there she was in the bright light, just as beautiful as he remembered her.

6

He remembered. Anne Freux had promised to wait ten years for him.

"I'm asking you for ten years," said Martin. "It could be less if I'm lucky. If not, I've calculated it will take me ten years."

Anne swore that she would wait for him. She tearfully kissed him. She was sixteen and a half. Martin was eighteen—tall, strong, stupid, and calculating. His calculations weren't intelligent, either.

He said goodbye to Dédé that same night. He said nothing to his father. Charles Terrier had arrived in Nauzac a little after the Second World War, accompanied by his pregnant wife and his pal Dédé. The two men had just made themselves a little nest egg in scrap and rags, especially in the salvaging of non-ferrous metals. That was the era when junk dealers, large and small, most of them Auvergnats, were battling to see who would salvage the most military surplus. They greased palms, schemed, often stole from one another, sometimes even exchanged gunshots. Charles Terrier took a Mauser rifle bullet in the head, and it stayed there, sometimes provoking a kind of attack, especially if he had been drinking. He stopped drinking. According to Dédé, he had been a pretty clever fellow before his wound. Then he married a nag and let Dédé convince him to leave the Paris area—where things had started to get too hot for them in variety of ways—and move to the Southwest to get into the mink-raising business.

"A clean life," said Dédé. "You'll be your old self again."

The minks died, the money was lost, Martin was born, and his mother packed up and left with a truck driver who had spent two days in Nauzac on account of a busted axle. The mother left Martin behind. Charles Terrier brought up the kid the hard way. Dédé also took care of the kid, and he was more affable and easygoing. Later, when Charles Terrier wanted to put his son to work, it was Dédé who convinced him to send the kid to the lycée, instead. It was also Dédé who took Martin to Paris one weekend for his sixteenth birthday and got him initiated by a prostitute in the vicinity of the Madeleine. He gave him a moped, too.

At the lycée, Martin hung out with bourgeois kids who borrowed his moped. It was the moped that got him in with the children of the rich, and then he fell madly in love with Anne Freux, who had expensive clothes and sheer dark stockings and wore Guerlain perfumes.

Everyone wanted to get Anne Freux, who just laughed, tossed her hair, and slipped out of reach. Martin paid rather a lot for a mail-order muscle-building course. But he had no success with the girls of the group, who found him a little vulgar. He made up for it elsewhere; he even had an affair with a girl working for the Freux company. But a girl like that didn't satisfy his imagination.

Nevertheless, one Saturday evening when Anne had asked him to take her home after a party where they had danced to Miles Davis, she and he kissed violently, then Martin said that if she'd asked him to take her home it was only to get rid of the others. She was indignant. He said he was embarrassed at his humble origins, and she was indignant again. She said that she found Martin much more colorful than the others, and she said that it was precisely because of his social background and because the others were spoiled children, but not him—he was acquainted with real-life problems, he worked in the summer instead of going on vacation, he had to struggle to elevate himself, and all that, she said finally, made him deeper and more mature.

But when Martin slipped his tongue in her mouth, she seemed surprised, and when he tried to feel her up, she pulled away and said good night and disappeared, a little flushed, into the posh little apartment house that would later have a West Indian concierge.

The following Saturday, Martin told her he loved her. Then things moved along at their own pace. During summer vacation, Anne often didn't answer the letters from Martin, who had remained in Nauzac to work. But at summer's end, she kissed more enthusiastically and accepted more daring caresses. And at the beginning of October, to his astonishment, Martin was invited to dinner at the Freux's. For the occasion, he wore a tie and borrowed a shirt and cuff links from his father. Submitted to a running fire of questions by the Freux parents, he answered clumsily and mishandled the silverware. Tipsy from drinking white wine followed by red, he became voluble at the end of the meal, and his vocabulary deteriorated.

After dinner, the elder Freux led him into his study. He gave the young man to understand that he did not have a brilliant future and that Anne would one day marry a man from her milieu. In conclusion, he ordered Martin never to see his daughter again and sent the adolescent out by the service stairs.

That evening, blind with rage and humiliation, Martin almost hit his father because Charles Terrier was drunk and looking for a fight about the borrowed shirt and cuff links. Fortunately, the father had one of his fits before things went seriously to hell.

Charles Terrier had begun drinking again a while before. Friends of Martin's, guys from his little crowd, had bought Charles a drink at the brasserie where he was a waiter, and they found the resulting rapid disturbance in the employee's behavior very funny. They came back on other days to buy him more drinks. They began calling Charles Terrier "Charlie Chaplin."

When the waiter was dismissed for his misbehavior, the young smart alecks surrounded him, alternately shamefaced and condescending. They went barhopping with him. As soon as Charles Terrier was drunk again, his foolishness started up even worse than before. In the wee hours, the man was overcome with uncontrollable anger. The last smart asses dispersed. Charles Terrier wandered the empty streets shouting that he wanted to leave town, and then he stole a motorcycle and, at the first turn, lost his balance and smashed his skull against the curb.

"I will return, I will kill them, I will drag them through the shit, I will make them eat shit," said Martin Terrier to Dédé at dawn after he had kissed Anne and she had sworn to wait ten years.

Even if his father had not been dead, Martin would have had nothing to say to him. He took a train that morning without waiting for the burial. He got as far as Toulouse, where he joined the army.

7

He also remembered this:

"And you, you have nothing to say?" asked the Italian woman journalist.

Terrier shrugged his shoulders.

"I have nothing interesting to say."

The other two white soldiers had just been going on about their origins, their taste for combat, and also, after a certain amount of persuading, their ideological convictions and the fact that someone really had to oppose the communist penetration of Africa. One of the fellows was English, the other German. They and Terrier and the journalist, along with the bearded black man with the cultivated look who was accompanying the journalist and wearing a government uniform without insignia, were in the devastated lounge of a solid-looking hotel. The ventilators were out of order, and the windows were broken; there was a lot of excrement behind the bar, even though the john was only two meters from the counter. Beyond the broken panes, the dusty street was deserted and bleached by the sun. In the middle of it lay the corpse of a fifteen-year-old rebel in shorts whom government troops had beaten to death just before the journalist arrived. Sporadic firing could be heard a kilometer or two away.

Since the journalist was looking at him with interest, Terrier said with embarrassment that he had the same kind of past as the other two, except that he had done his normal national service, in France, in the paratroops.

"And you like to fight?"

"Not especially."

"Why are you here? Out of conviction?"

The journalist took notes on a small pad. She had short blond hair and black eyes. She was rather tall, plump, dressed in combat fatigues, desirable. You could see her tongue move between her white teeth when she spoke.

"No," said Terrier, with embarrassment. "I do it only for the money."

"That's interesting," said the journalist, looking interested. "You and your colleagues always begin by saying it's only for the money. But if you scratch the surface, you discover things. In fact, I would love to find someone who is here only for the money." She spoke impeccable French. "But I don't believe it. Still, I would like to. I mean, risking your life just for the money, is that possible, you know what I mean? I wonder." She tapped her white incisors with her pencil.

"What I was saying is, I have a life plan," mumbled Terrier.

"A life plan?" The Italian arched her eyebrows.

"Drop it. Uh, drop it," said Terrier.

He caught the eye of the bearded black man whose uniform carried no markings. The black man smiled slightly.

"No," said the Italian. "A life plan?"

"Shit," said Terrier. "I want to build up a fund. I've given myself ten years. Then I'll hang it up and go into something else."

"Go into what?"

"That's none of your business, madame."

The Italian looked at him with a smile, and her black eyes were laughing, too, and perhaps enticing. The door of the john slammed open. A thirteen-year-old black male dressed only in khaki shorts and a red helmet jumped out howling as he opened fire on the group.

In five seconds, there were some fifteen, maybe seventeen

shots. When silence returned, the German, the Englishman, and the Italian were flat on the floor. The adolescent sniper was sitting against the doorjamb of the john, dead; he had lost his red helmet and had holes through the heart and face. Terrier and the black man with the cultivated look were standing, still tightly grasping their warm automatic pistols in both hands. They looked each other over and exchanged slight smiles. The people who were flat on the floor began to get back up, their faces ashen. The black man in the uniform with no markings relaxed, gave Terrier a tap on the shoulder, walked over to the corpse, and picked up the gun.

"I'd like to know just which fuckers are supplying them with Armalites," he said. He, too, spoke perfect French.

Terrier wanted to say something in reply, but his right leg collapsed under him. He found himself sitting on the floor. He shook his head. His thigh hurt. Blood spurted from it.

"Pressure dressing," he managed to say.

Later, he was in a hotel bed, swollen up and feverish. The shutters were closed behind the open window. There was artillery fire in the distance, perhaps ten kilometers away. Stanley, the black man, was sitting at his bedside with lemons and a bottle of vodka; smiling, he studied Terrier. Stanley's skin was very black, to the point where he was almost invisible in the darkness when he wasn't smiling. Between the artillery reports dreadful wailing could be heard. It sounded like a prisoner under torture. But when one listened more closely, it turned out to be only the Italian journalist getting it on with some guy.

"The war's over for you," said Stanley. "That thigh will take a good month. So do you have any plans?"

"No."

"I have a proposition for you," said Stanley. "I really liked the way you reacted this morning."

"What?" Terrier didn't really understand.

"All the others, on the floor," said Stanley.

"Oh, yes," muttered Terrier. "Yes."

"I have a proposition."

And that was where and how Martin Terrier was recruited.

8

Anne Freux, Schrader's wife, shook her head when Terrier handed her the fruit bowl. She got up from the table and dropped into an armchair in a corner of the room, where she inhaled her Kent and stared into space. Terrier picked up an orange and set about peeling it fastidiously with a knife and fork. Félix Schrader watched him with a fascinated and amused look.

"What have you been doing, exactly?"

"Employee relations," said Terrier. "A big firm."

"You've seen something of the world."

Terrier raised his gaze from the orange for a moment and caught Félix's look of amusement.

"A little."

Félix got up, went through the open glass double door, and foraged in the shadows of the adjoining study. Bound volumes covered the walls. He worked a drawer and returned to the well-lighted dining room with a shoe box. Anne jerked her head; her lips tightened a little. Félix opened the box and turned it over on the tablecloth. Some twelve or fifteen postcards poured out. They had been mailed from a great variety of places: Nairobi, Geneva, Los Angeles, Colombo, Kyoto, Berlin, Tripoli, Manaus, and other spots. There was no text, only the name of Mademoiselle Anne Freux and her old address.

"You're the one who sent all these?" asked Félix.

"Uh, well," said Terrier. "Uh, well, yes."

"I thought you'd thrown them out," Anne said, without looking at Félix.

Her husband smiled at her. She lighted a new cigarette from the butt of the preceding one. She got up, opened a small glass sideboard, and poured herself a good twenty centiliters of Martell in a snifter.

"Don't you think you've had enough to drink today?" asked Félix.

"Shit."

Anne sat violently back down. She was a rather tall, well-proportioned young woman with plump breasts, a generous mouth, very light green eyes, pale complexion, and blond hair. Her eyes seemed to express not the slightest thought. Fine lines were apparent at the corners of her eyes and mouth. She took a healthy swig of her cognac.

"I've come to take Anne away," Terrier said suddenly, putting his napkin down.

Standing with his spread fingers pressed against the table, Félix half smiled in a reflective way.

"You shouldn't be speaking to me. Speak to the lady."

Terrier got up. He stumbled imperceptibly.

"Anne," he said.

Anne stood up and drained her cognac.

"I'm sleepy. I'm going up." She slurred her words a little.

"Anne," repeated Terrier. "Anne, for God's sake!"

The young woman left the room without looking at anyone. Terrier moved to catch up with her. Félix took a half step to the side. Terrier almost bumped into him.

"Shall I make us coffee?" suggested Félix. "I have an Italian machine that makes fantastic coffee. Do you know how to play Mastermind?"

"What?" Terrier looked at him as if he were crazy.

"Coffee?" Félix repeated affably. He had black eyes and black hair and a Latin face with a dull complexion, slightly protruding cheekbones, and a long, slightly hooked nose; he was smaller in size and stature than Terrier and seemed three or four years younger; he wore gray corduroy pants, a sport shirt, and a woolen smoking jacket. "So you don't want any of my coffee?" he said, putting on an expression of comical disappointment.

"Shit, no, you can't be for real!" exclaimed Terrier. Terrier raised his forearms, then brought his fists down to his thighs, sighed, moved back a step, shook his head, and seemed to calm down.

"What's the matter? What's the matter?" asked Félix. "Do you want my advice? Do you need my advice? Is that it? Is that it? I don't give a damn! I don't give a damn!" he shouted. Then he added calmly: "If there's anything wrong, it's your head!"

Terrier advanced blindly and with his outstretched right arm tried to push Félix out of the way. Félix retreated.

"I want to talk to Anne," said Terrier.

"She's drunk. She's sleeping. She's snoring." He snickered.

Terrier slapped Félix's mouth full force with the back of his hand. Félix backed away again.

"Come spend the weekend," he said. He touched a finger to his lip and then examined the end of his finger. "Do you remember the cabin? We often spend the weekend there. We're going this weekend. Come up Saturday, okay?"

Terrier stared at him.

"Hey!" laughed Félix. "You want to knock me off or what?"

"Excuse me," whispered Terrier.

"You're excused." Félix gave Terrier's arm a pat. "It's an embarrassing situation for you. Well, actually, no. Anyway, screw it!" He turned his back to Terrier. "So you don't want my coffee? Would you care for a liqueur? You don't want to play Mastermind with me? Maybe Saturday?"

"Maybe," murmured Terrier.

He turned around and quickly reached the door, grabbing his leather coat on his way down the hall. He got in the DS, drove off rapidly, and returned to his hotel. It was midnight.

"Someone brought a package for you," said the clerk in the burgundy jacket as he handed Terrier his key.

"Give it to me."

"The chambermaid took it up."

"Well, fine," said Terrier.

"It was awfully heavy," the clerk ventured as Terrier was getting into the narrow elevator.

After unlocking the door to his room, Terrier slowly opened it with his foot, turned on the lights, and suspiciously examined the room and the enormous package tied up with ribbons. After a moment, he went inside and locked the door. He glanced inside the armoire and the bathroom. Then he circled the package and scrutinized it from all sides. He dug in his suitcase and pulled out an Opinel knife. Squatting before the package, he made little pokes with the blade into the wrapping paper and bumped something hard everywhere. He cut the ribbons and then, still using the blade of the Opinel knife, slit the paper and began to tear pieces off. Metal and plastic corners appeared along with transparent glass surfaces, behind which indistinct forms could be made out. Terrier finished tearing off the paper.

Inside the package was a sealed aquarium, full of water. In the aquarium floated the tomcat Sudan, gutted, his eyes ripped out and his intestines undulating slowly in water dark with blood.

9

Terrier remained motionless for an instant, then he went and got the HK4's box from his suitcase; he opened the box on the bed. The various parts of the weapon were still there. The man again mounted the barrel chambered for .380 and put the automatic in his jacket pocket. Then he telephoned the desk and questioned the man in the burgundy jacket.

"Well," said the clerk, "the person didn't give a name, actually."

"Describe the person."

"Well, I don't know, the person concerned said that it had to be a surprise, actually, and not to, in fact. . . . "

"For Christ's sake!" exclaimed Terrier with impatience.

"Excuse me, monsieur," said the clerk, who seemed shocked and worried. "Is something the matter?"

"Everything's fine. Describe this person for me."

"It was a woman," said the clerk. "I don't know what to say. Short black hair in a helmet cut, a very popular style these days, with bangs, you know? Blue eyes, a fine long nose, a slightly drooping mouth, like Jeanne Moreau's, the actress, you know? And what else? Medium height, perhaps one meter sixty-three. A nylon navy-blue raincoat buttoned up to the neck and blue leather boots. She had a rain hat in her hand that matched her raincoat and . . . oh, she wore long, blue leather gloves. She was smoking a cork-tip cigarette. She gave me twenty francs in two ten-franc coins. That's all I remember. Oh, yes. If you don't mind my saying so, monsieur, she had dry skin. Pink cheeks, you see? As if her skin had peeled after a sunburn or she had bad circulation. Not that she had acne rosacea, because she was a woman in her thirties, but still. . . . Some Englishwomen and Scandinavians have this sort of coloring. I'm afraid I don't remember much else, actually. I'm not very observant, and I didn't pay close attention."

"I wonder what it would be like if you did!"

"Beg your pardon?" said the clerk.

"Nothing. She came and went by car?"

"I suppose so. I don't know."

"What's your name?"

"Philippe, monsieur."

"Well, Philippe," said Terrier, "let me know right away if this woman shows up again. There's a tip in it for you—in any case. And thanks."

"My pleasure, monsieur."

"Good night," said Terrier.

He hung up softly, shaking his head and smiling. Then his smile vanished. He returned to the opened package and completely freed the aquarium of its wrapping. As he did so, a card appeared bearing a hand-stenciled message in capital letters: "WITH THE COMPLIMENTS OF LUIGI ROSSI." Terrier carefully examined the card, then the wrapping paper and the ribbons, even holding them up to the light of the bedside lamp. After tearing the card into tiny pieces, he put everything in the wastebasket.

The man turned out the lights in the room and positioned himself near the window, observing the humid night and the yellowish glow that the ground-floor lights, reduced at the moment, cast on the front steps, the gravel paths, and a few dark, gleaming, motionless automobiles.

After putting the aquarium in the bottom of the armoire, closing the shutters, and drawing the curtains, Terrier slept, with the HK4 under the pillow, until close to eight in the morning.

As he drove away from the hotel, he discreetly observed his surroundings and the rearview mirror. Sometimes he drove very fast and sometimes times very slow. It seemed that he wasn't being followed.

At present, the public dump carried a sign that read "No Dumping," but on the slope was still the same mess of broken bottles, melon rinds, tin cans, rusty springs, dark rags, and dismembered celluloid baby dolls as before. Terrier stopped the DS on the adjacent flat area. When the road was empty, he threw the aquarium down the hill. It bounced once, then broke apart on the second impact and continued to tumble down, the plate glass shattering, with pieces of dead cat flying in every direction as the thing bounced and smashed and scattered its parts around the base of the cone of rubbish until they were just indistinct and motionless pieces of detritus.

Terrier got back behind the wheel of the DS and sat still for a moment, looking frequently in the rearview mirror. A few cars passed quickly on the wet highway. Nothing else happened.

Terrier got back on the road going the other way and returned to the center of Nauzac. From a telephone at the post office he dialed a Paris number.

"Where are you?" asked Stanley.

Terrier did not answer the question. He told Stanley as little as he could: he mentioned the phone calls before his departure from Paris, the ransacked apartment, the name of Luigi Rossi, the death of Alex, the cat.

"That's disgusting," said Stanley.

"Do you have any idea of what's going on?"

"No. You ought to come back, Christian."

"Try to find out."

"If you come back," said Stanley, "you'll have the protection of the company."

"Try to find out," repeated Terrier. "I'll call back."

He hung up and returned to his hotel.

There was a message for him: Anne had called, she would call back, no point in calling her because she would be out. Terrier gave a hundred francs to Philippe, the clerk.

"The tip I mentioned," he said. He looked at his watch. "Are you on duty twenty-four hours a day?"

"From seven in the morning till one in the morning," said the man in the burgundy jacket.

"You're going to wear yourself out."

"It's only temporary," said the clerk. "I'm ambitious."

Terrier nodded and went up to his room. He was sweating. He went into the bathroom and looked at the shower head, then went back into the room and looked at the telephone. Finally, he sat down with a glass full of a little scotch and a lot of tepid ginger ale. He immediately stood back up and went to rest his warm forehead against the icy glass of the window. He looked vaguely at the little park and the lawn. Right then, Anne pulled into the driveway, at the wheel of a Morris. Terrier watched her stop and get out of the little automobile. She came into the hotel. Terrier ripped off his shirt as he ran into the bathroom. He splashed himself with water, sprayed on deodorant, slipped on a clean white shirt. The telephone rang.

"Martin? It's me."

"Come right up."

"I'm calling from home," said Anne.

"That's not true," said Terrier. "You're in the lobby. Come

right up." With one hand he clumsily shoved his shirttails into his pants.

"Fine."

A moment later, someone knocked softly on the door.

"I'm not staying," Anne said right away as she slipped through the half-open door. Terrier locked the door. The young woman pivoted in the middle of the room and seemed to be examining the furniture; her eyes were expressionless. "I'm not staying," she repeated. "I only wanted to tell you. . . . I want you to stop imagining that. . . ." She hesitated. "Can I have something to drink?"

Terrier poured her a drink. She gulped down a straight shot, then clicked her tongue as she held out her glass for some ginger ale from the little bottle he was holding. He poured her some. He cast furtive glances at her through half-closed eyes, like a lizard in the sun.

"I came to tell you," Anne explained. "We're not kids anymore." She emptied her glass.

Terrier gave her an ironic smile and poured her a stiff shot of J&B. Anne sighed and sat down on the bed. She took a sip. Terrier sat down next to her, took her by the head, and kissed her. She let him do it. Her mouth was passive, studious, plump, and tasted like scotch.

"Stop," she whispered after Terrier released her.

"Undress."

She took off almost all her clothes.

"The panties, too," said Terrier.

She took off her panties, got into bed, and turned to the wall, her eyes closed. Terrier undressed quickly, almost fell as he removed his socks, and joined her in bed. He didn't dare touch Anne because his hands were cold. They kept still for a moment. Terrier realized he was losing his erection. He tried to put a hand on the young woman's hip, but she pushed him away with her elbow and climbed over the man and leaped out of bed. She grabbed her clothes and disappeared into the bathroom, locking the door behind her. Terrier got dressed and lit a Gauloise. His cold hands were trembling. Anne reappeared, completely clothed.

"I should go home," she said. "Anyway, this wasn't serious."

Terrier said nothing in response. The muscles around his mouth were taut. Anne picked her glass up from the floor and emptied it, then she rushed from the room. Her cheeks were red.

10

After finishing his cigarette, Terrier took a shower. Then he left the hotel by car and headed for a deserted place in the mountains, an abandoned quarry, where he practiced firing the HK4. He returned to the hotel and drank eight scotches. His cheeks and the area around his eyes were red. At ten-thirty he left the hotel again and went to the Brasserie des Fleurs.

The place was full of light and heat. Smiling, Terrier sat down at a small table, not far from a redhead in a green dress whom he had noticed as he came in. She was pretty and plump, with a head of curly hair and heavy arms that were pale, soft, and smooth. Two guys were with her, huddling together to tell each other jokes and laughing noisily. Terrier ordered the special. It wasn't Dédé who served him; Dédé was taking care of another part of the room and didn't notice him. Terrier observed the redhead as he ate. The special was surprisingly disgusting.

At the end of the meal, after downing two cognacs, Terrier tossed some bills on the table and stumbled slightly as he made his way over to the redhead. She watched him approach. She was licking melted sugar from the bottom of her coffee cup with her red tongue.

"Would you come outside with me for a minute?" Terrier asked her. "I would like to speak to you."

"Go sleep it off somewhere else, friend," said one of her companions.

Terrier picked up the speaker's coffee cup and emptied it on his head. He was a skinny dark young guy dressed in a checked suit. Dédé had noticed Terrier and was on his way over, looking worried and with a round tray under his left arm. The young guy knocked over his chair as he stood up, raising his fists, with coffee dribbling down his face. The redhead broke into a slow laugh and bit her knuckles. Terrier slapped his open palms against the skinny guy's ears. Grimacing, his eyes shut, the young guy fell to his knees and brought his hands to his ears. He gritted his teeth to stop himself from screaming. Tears sprang from the corners of his eyes. His companion half rose, then slowly sat back down.

"Are you looking for trouble?" asked Terrier.

The other man shook his head. A watery-eyed Dédé had halted a little way off, shaking his head. The diners nearby were covertly observing the scene.

"Let's go get your coat," Terrier said to the redhead.

"What if I don't want to?" she asked, getting up. "I don't have a coat, anyway."

Terrier took her arm and guided her away. She threw her head back and smiled. They had to pass Dédé on their way out.

"So you're going to start acting like your old man, huh?" said the old waiter as they went by.

Later, Terrier awoke in a messy bed that was just a big mattress on the floor with sheets and a blanket in a big white room plunged in darkness (but through the slats of the shutters daylight could be seen). The man's clothing lay strewn about and crumpled on the cheap carpet. There were long twisted butts on a plate full of ashes, a poster of Marlon Brando in *The Wild One* hung on the wall, and a turntable softly played Brian Ferry's "Tokyo Joe." Terrier checked his wristwatch. Two o'clock in the afternoon. Certainly not two o'clock in the morning. Engines were running outside; inside the building children were crying and television sets were going. The man got up and pulled on his briefs. The redhead came into the room and pointed the HK4 at him. Terrier was three meters away from her. He blinked and stayed absolutely still.

Smiling, the redhead came closer, aiming the HK4. When she came within two meters, Terrier grabbed his jacket by the collar from the back of a chair and swept the air with this article of clothing, striking the automatic and the girl's wrist. The weapon flew out of her hands. At the same moment, Terrier dove full length onto the floor and grabbed the redhead's ankles. He made her fall on her back. The girl's head collided with the cheap carpet.

"Ow! You're nuts!" she complained as she tried to get back up.

Terrier had retrieved the automatic and, with one knee on the floor, was aiming it with two hands at the head of red hair. He noticed that the safety was on. He relaxed a little.

"Shit, you hurt me! Shit on you!" The girl was sitting up on the floor with legs spread and massaging her curly head.

"Sorry," said Terrier. "You scared me."

He stood up and stuffed the HK4 into a jacket pocket.

"I didn't go through your pockets," said the redhead, who was getting back up while still rubbing her skull, but now with only one hand. "I was looking for cigarettes. What is that thing? Are you a crook?"

In the darkness, her heavily made-up eyes and mouth formed three spots or three holes in her white face. She was wearing a black acrylic dressing gown decorated with Chinese ideograms in red.

"No. Don't worry about it."

"I'm not worried."

A kettle whistled in the kitchen.

"May I?" asked the girl.

"Sure."

She left and came back in with a tray, cups, sugar, Nescafé, and the kettle. Meanwhile, Terrier had put his clothes back on. The girl raised the blinds a little to brighten the room.

"It's a defensive weapon," said Terrier. "For my job."

"And just what is your job, if I may ask?"

"Business. Sometimes I have to carry a lot of money. And you?"

"I'm in electricity," said the girl. She sat down cross-legged near the tray and made coffee in the cups. "Yes, well, shit, I'm a worker, to be more precise. I assemble record players."

"I've already met someone like you before," said Terrier.

"There's no shortage."

"Tell me, did we fuck last night?" asked Terrier.

"Only a little. You don't remember?"

"Not really. Was I good?"

"You were loaded."

"But for a guy who was loaded, was I good?"

"You piss me off," the girl said.

"Come to bed."

"Oh, no!" exclaimed the girl. "It's my Saturday. I have one Saturday per month."

"Saturday," repeated Terrier. "Saturday? Oh, yeah."

He got up and left.

11

"I talked a little with Anne," Félix said affably. "She's annoyed because she doesn't know how to make you understand that she doesn't want you."

Terrier said nothing in response. Félix emptied his glass.

"I like whisky sours because they taste like vomit," he said, looking malevolently at Terrier. (Félix seemed to have already had a lot to drink.)

The two men were seated in bamboo armchairs on the terrace of the so-called cabin—actually, a rather spacious wooden chalet, planted on a steep, wooded hill some hundred kilometers from Nauzac. The Atlantic was visible between the pine trees. The ocean was iron gray, and the whitish sky was turning darker. There was little wind. It was cold, but less so than inland. Félix was wearing jeans and boots and a thick white ribbed sweater of virgin wool. He had offered to lend Terrier a pullover, but Terrier had refused and sat stiffly in his suit. His back didn't touch the back of the chair; the tips of his elbows were on the armrests; his hands were clasped around his nearly full cylindrical glass.

"If you systematically drink something that tastes like vomit," continued Félix, "you won't be confused when you end up vomiting."

The two men were looking attentively at each other. Félix was smiling; Terrier was not. Near the low table with its cane top was one more armchair, an empty one. Anne came back from inside the house with a silver cocktail shaker and sat down in the chair. She was wearing a thick loose sweater, corduroy trousers, and red boots. She refilled her husband's glass, then served herself. She glanced at Terrier, then looked down at the ground.

"We regularly come here because there's nothing to do in Nauzac," declared Félix. "What a hole! Two photography exhibitions per year, domino tournaments, things like that. An undubbed foreign film the first Monday of every month, at midnight—you get the idea. Have you seen the latest Altman?"

"What?" said Terrier.

"The latest Altman. Robert Altman."

"He's a film director," Anne explained. She was looking up now; the sky was turning darker than the sea; it was twilight.

"What do you think of Régis Debray's position on the media and intellectuals?" asked Félix, giving Terrier a mean look. "What do you think of the new French crime novel? And do you think that jazz can still progress? Personally, I have my doubts when I see Archie Shepp practically return to bebop if not to Ben Webster, or when I see a guy like Anthony Braxton hailing Lee Konitz, or when I see what's become of guys who once showed such promise, like Marion Brown or, more in our line, Chico Freeman. Between meaninglessness and suffering, I prefer bacon, as the Auvergnats say. No, seriously, it's frivolity on one side and boredom on the other, and I say fuck it. Of course, I'm well aware that these are aspects of the same crisis. Don't you agree?"

Félix noisily caught his breath. Terrier was frowning.

"I don't know," said Terrier.

"Stop bullshitting, Félix," Anne murmured distractedly.

"So what do you like?" Félix mockingly asked Terrier. He glanced at Anne and looked back at Terrier, who was perplexed. "In music, for example."

Terrier shrugged. Félix brought his glass to his lips and emptied it at one go.

"Maria Callas," said Terrier.

Félix had a choking fit. He coughed, spat up his whisky sour all over his chin and his sweater, stood up desperately gasping for breath and whistling like a fife, coughed again and stumbled as he circled the table, stamping his heels on the terrace floor in an apparent attempt to clear his bronchial tubes and trachea. Anne looked at Terrier, who got up and thumped Félix's back. Then the young woman suddenly turned her head toward the interior of the little house because there had been a small crash, as if a breakable object had fallen on the kitchen floor. Anne left the terrace while Félix was trying, with difficulty, to catch his breath. His face was flushed; tears streamed from his eyes.

"But you're not for real," he said to Terrier in a weak, halting voice. He had trouble pulling a vast white handkerchief out of the pocket of his tight jeans; he dabbed his eyes and chin and then the front of his sweater with it. "You're a fool," he asserted, wonderment in his voice. "That's it. You'd have to be a fool to go away for ten years and imagine. . . . " He broke off with a little gesture and a little laugh. "As for money, I didn't have any more than you in terms of personal money. But I'm intelligent. I'm not a fool like you. A lot of good that does me, mind you."

Terrier put his fists in his jacket pockets and stiffened his arms, which made him pull his head down between his oddly raised shoulders. He had the posture of a man fighting against the cold or against a disagreeable emotion.

Félix smiled nastily and sadly as he looked off into space.

"What I have belongs to me," he whispered, still hoarse and panting. "It's not for you. That's the way it is. There's no mistake." He frowned; he seemed to be thinking hard. "No, there's been no mistake," he concluded firmly.

"Dinner's ready!" shouted Anne from inside the house.

"We're coming!" Félix shouted back. He looked at his watch and said in a low voice: "Shit, what's the matter with her? I'm not hungry yet."

Terrier took his hands out of his pockets, turned his back to Félix, and went into the house, going directly into the vast main room, where there was a dining nook, a living area, and a convertible sofa where visiting friends could sleep. The walls were made of rough boards coated with a clear varnish, most of the furniture was rustic and old, and here and there old copper utensils decorated the place. In the hearth burned a wood fire that Félix had lighted a little while before and stoked with a copper toasting fork some sixty centimeters long that he had purchased the year before at an antiques shop in Ireland. Terrier took a deep breath. After emptying what remained of the whisky sour in his glass, Félix followed him in.

"What's going on? The table's not even set!" he exclaimed in the direction of the half-open door of the kitchen.

The door opened completely, revealing Anne. A dark young woman with a Louise Brooks cut, her cheeks slightly blotchy, in a navy blue nylon raincoat, was holding Anne's blond hair in her left hand and with her right sticking the short barrel of a Colt Special Agent revolver in her ear.

"Stop right there," she said.

Terrier came to an instant halt. Félix took one more step and stopped, his mouth forming an O and his eyes blinking. Astonishment or alcohol made him totter a bit.

"Hey, look," he said in a half-choked voice.

"Silence," said a man's voice.

Two guys had stolen across the terrace; they entered the

room. The shorter was also the fatter. His beige fur-lined jacket was stretched over his belly; a brown Tyrolean hat was perched on his bald round head. He wore glasses and had an awful complexion riddled with tiny craters and blackheads. He quickly and very carefully frisked Terrier without finding a weapon.

Meanwhile, the other man—who was thin, no older than twenty-two or twenty-three, with longish glistening black hair, fleshy lips, and the soft pretty face of a pimp or a faggot—was closing the shutters. He wore a khaki hunting jacket and a khaki sun hat pulled well down. As he was fastening the last shutter, the other man, the short fat one, turned on the lights. Terrier drew imperceptibly closer to Félix.

"There's a pistol in my leather coat," he whispered under the racket made by the closing shutter.

"No whispering!" commanded the brunette with the Colt. She released Anne's hair and, with a shove, sent the young woman stumbling into the middle of the room. "Everyone sit down on the floor with their hands on their heads!"

Terrier and Anne obeyed immediately. Félix put one knee on the floor, with his hands half raised and a nervous smile playing around the corners of his mouth.

"What is this?" he asked, stuttering a little. "Is this a holdup?"

The brunette took three steps forward and smashed his nose with the barrel of her revolver. Félix let out a horrified cry and tried to get back up. The girl struck the base of his skull with the Colt, and the thin young man booted him in the small of the back. Félix rolled and moaned on the floor. He closed one hand over his smashed nose. Blood ran from his nose and from his opened scalp.

"Leave him alone. He's a nitwit," declared Terrier.

He remained motionless, sitting on the floor with his hands on his head, as instructed. The brunette looked at him unsmilingly. She slipped behind Terrier, stuck her Colt in the pocket of her raincoat, grabbed his left hand and pulled back his little finger. The joint gave way with a dry crack. Terrier gave out a long, violent groan through his closed mouth, his chest heaving and tears bursting from his closed eyes, then he suddenly puked a little of the whisky sour over his knees.

"Compared with what we're going to do to you if you annoy us, that's nothing," declared the brunette. She moved around to look Terrier in the face. "I'm Rossana Rossi," she said. "And you are Martin Terrier. Some people call you Christian. Five years ago, you killed my brother. You're going to tell me about that."

"Tie up the other two and stow them upstairs, and we'll talk," said Terrier.

"It doesn't matter anymore—they know my name."

"Yes!" shouted Félix. "Yes, it matters! We don't know anything, we don't want to know anything—settle your business between yourselves! Tie us up and lock us up upstairs and settle things between yourselves! Listen, I've already forgotten your name. Listen, I can prove my good faith: Terrier has a gun. I can tell you where!"

Anne turned toward Félix and sized him up. He was pitiful and pathetic with his hair sticky with blood and the mixture of blood, tears, and mucus that trickled from his nose. Rossana Rossi was also looking at Félix.

"In his leather coat," said Félix. "On the coat rack over there." With an indistinct movement of his head, he indicated the rack where Terrier's leather coat hung, at the far end of the room. "The hell with you, you stupid jerk," added Félix for the benefit of Terrier, who was not looking at him. Then Anne's husband closed his eyes and carefully palpated his nose. "I can't breathe anymore except through my mouth!" he whined.

The short fat man, a CZ automatic dangling from the end of his pudgy arm, exchanged glances with Rossana Rossi, nodded his head, and crossed the room. He found the HK4 in the outside pocket of the leather coat and came back, fiddling with the weapon with a contented look. The brunette brought her gaze back to Terrier.

"Well, then?" she said.

"Tie them up and take them upstairs."

"We're wasting time," said the brunette.

"He's right!" proclaimed Félix. "Take us upstairs! We don't have anything to do with your fucking problems!"

"Kill him," the brunette said to the short fat man, who pocketed his CZ and worked the action of the HK4.

"Wait, you're crazy!" shouted Félix. "Wait, Terrier is in love with my wife! Take me upstairs and keep my wife to make him talk!"

He gave Rossana Rossi a supplicating look. She half smiled. Terrier had closed his eyes; he gave a long sigh. The short fat man glanced at the brunette. She nodded, and he aimed the HK4 at Félix Schrader's head and pulled the trigger. The weapon made considerable noise in the enclosed room. Félix's head exploded. Organic debris flew in several directions and splattered against the walls and windows. Félix's corpse collapsed all at once on its side, with a thud. The smell of cordite hung in the air.

Terrier looked at Anne. She seemed absolutely calm, except that she had sunk her teeth into her lower lip.

"Ducio," the brunette said to the young guy, "look around, there must be candles somewhere in this shack. Find me a candle." Her hands were in the pockets of her raincoat. She leaned slightly toward Terrier. "We're going to put a candle in cutie pie's vagina," she announced with seeming affability.

"I killed your brother with a carbine, on a road in northern Italy," said Terrier. "I don't remember the date. What else do you want to know?"

The man called Ducio had gone into the kitchen where he was opening drawers and dumping their contents on the floor.

"We'd like to know why."

"I can't go on," Anne said suddenly. She rolled on the ground, emitting sharp little groans. Her limbs trembled. Her eyes turned up, and her teeth were bared. Her convulsions moved her almost a meter on her back, and then her body relaxed and she began breathing deeply. The whites of her eyes were visible between her lids. She stopped moving.

"How did you find me?" asked Terrier.

Rossana Rossi shook her head.

"You'll die without knowing. That's harder," she said. "We'll finish you and cutie pie off quickly if you tell us everything."

"I killed a certain number of people in recent years because I was ordered to," said Terrier. "I worked regularly for a guy by the name of Cox. An American. That's all I know."

"No. You obviously know a lot more than that."

Terrier sighed and began giving a rather exact physical description of Cox. There was dribble at the corners of Anne's mouth. Her convulsions had brought her close to the fireplace, where no one was paying her any mind. She suddenly got up and grabbed the long toasting fork in the hearth. Holding the utensil with both hands, she charged Rossana Rossi. Anne was screaming.

She was so fast that she reached the brunette before the woman could even begin to turn around. The three giant tines of the fork, entering under a shoulder blade, ran through one of the Italian's lungs.

Terrier jumped instantly to his feet and wrenched the Colt Special Agent from Rosanna Rossi's hand. A geyser of foaming blood was spurting from her mouth. When the two women fell flat on their bellies, one on top of the other, Terrier and the short fat man opened fire at the same time. The short fat man missed Terrier. A .38 caliber bullet burst the fat man's heart, and he fell. Terrier turned toward the kitchen, where the panic-stricken young guy was clumsily pulling a Savage automatic from his pocket. Terrier put a bullet in his stomach. Ducio dropped his automatic and fell to his knees, wailing. He caught hold of the kitchen door and slammed it shut. Terrier emptied the Colt through the door, then ran toward the terrace, picking up the HK4 on his way. He went out of the house, raced around to the other side as fast as he could, slipping in the pine needles and sand, and went up to the broken kitchen window. In the ravaged room, the man called Ducio leaned against the kitchen door. In his back were two craters the size of tomatoes. Hanging on to the doorknob, he was still trying to get up. Terrier entered the kitchen through the window. He picked up the Savage automatic and put it in his pocket, seized Ducio by his hair, and pulled him away from the door before going back into the living room.

The short fat man was dead, the two women unconscious. Terrier quickly examined Anne, noted that she had no physical wound, picked her up, and carried her to the convertible sofa. He hurried back to the kitchen. The young Italian was dead. Terrier returned to the living room, took out his handkerchief, and mopped his brow. His lips were trembling. After a moment, they stopped trembling. Then he saw that Anne had opened her eyes and was looking at him.

"I have to go," he said. "You have to say that you were upstairs, that you saw nothing, heard nothing. No, you heard gunshots, you came down, you found everyone dead. . . . "

"I'm going with you," Anne cut in.

For a moment, Terrier seemed incapable of formulating an answer.

"You don't have to," he said. "You just have to say . . ."

She interrupted again: "I'm going with you. Isn't that what you want?"

"Yes," said Terrier. "Yes."

He turned on his heel, striking his left palm with his right fist.

"Wait," he said. "I'd like you to go upstairs for a minute. You must . . . I should. . . . " He leaned over Rosanna Rossi and saw that she was dead. "No," he said. "Okay. Let's go."

12

They passed a police van, an Estafette, on the shoreline road.

"The neighbors must have heard something," said Terrier.

He glanced at Anne. She didn't seem in shock. She was sitting in a relaxed manner. She was looking straight ahead. There was a black spot on her lower lip, where she'd bitten it and made it bleed. She didn't respond.

"I can't run the risk of stopping back at my hotel or your house," said Terrier after a moment. "But I could drop you in the center of Nauzac."

"No."

"Or I can get right on the highway, and we head for Paris."

The young woman gave a small quick nod.

"You're sure you know what you're doing?"

"Yes!" she said. "Do you want something to drink?"

"No," said Terrier.

Anne turned around awkwardly under her seatbelt to grab the bottle of Martell cognac from the backseat. Before leaving, Terrier had collected all the handguns, abandoning the automatic weapons, an M16 and an Uzi, where he had found them: in the Rossi clan's car, a BMW parked under the pine trees about a hundred meters from the house. After making a hesitant tour of the premises, Anne had merely slipped on her wolf-skin coat and taken the cognac. She pulled out the cork and brought the neck to her lips, but then she put the bottle back on her lap.

"Not that thirsty," she said. She corked the bottle and put it on the floorboard, between her feet. She looked at Terrier. "Would you rather people didn't talk to you while you're driving?"

"That doesn't bother me." They had now reached a main road. Terrier slowed down, switched on his turn indicator, and took the junction leading to the highway. His broken finger did not seem to impede his driving.

"Did you really kill people all those years?"

"Oh," said Terrier. "You heard that."

"Of course," Anne said deliberately. "I didn't black out or have a fit when I rolled on the floor. I wanted to get closer to that damn fork." She shivered. "Somebody had to do something. They would have killed us, right?" She frowned. Her face was no longer expressionless. On the contrary, it was serious: she seemed to be concentrating. "I've never seen such people," she said. "Are you like them? Or not?" Suddenly, her voice and her look became uncertain again.

"I'm like them. Not only. But I'm like them."

"They weren't only like that, either, I suppose," said Anne. She chuckled out of pure nervousness. "What I just said was very philosophical."

"No doubt."

Road signs announcing the proximity of the highway went by very quickly to the right of the DS. In fact, out of the night appeared a zone of orange half-light where the curves of an empty interchange meandered beneath overhead traffic signs. Entry to the toll road was not automated: there was a glass booth.

"Turn up your collar, turn toward your door, and don't move," Terrier ordered.

Anne obeyed. The DS halted near the glass cabin. A yawning, ruddy-faced employee gave Terrier a ticket through the driver's window. The car started up, went down the ramp, gathered speed on the access lane, then, its turn indicator flashing, slipped onto the highway nearly devoid of traffic. It was almost midnight.

"Are you, uh, what they call a crook?" Anne asked after a few minutes.

"A crook?" repeated Terrier. "I don't think you say that much anymore. Well, no. No, I'm not a bandit." He hesitated. "Listen, I was a soldier of fortune—a mercenary, if you like."

Anne remained silent for so long that Terrier believed that she had no comment to make. But then she spoke:

"Not necessarily within the framework of normal military operations and not necessarily in uniform, is that it?"

"That's it."

"And who is this American named Cox?"

"Forget that," said Terrier. "Forget that right now."

"Fine," said Anne. "As much as I can. Do you plan to stop somewhere, or are we going to keep on charging along until we fall into the Baltic and drown?"

"We're heading for Paris."

"Don't you think they'll set up roadblocks?"

"The police? It'll take them quite a while to identify me and the car," said Terrier. "If they are very efficient and act very quickly, they'll be in the know around midday. We'll arrive long before."

"And then?"

"There are any number of places that I can take you if you want to come along."

"For example?"

"Well," said Terrier, "what I had in mind at the beginning—I mean, before things went to hell, when I just thought I would show up and take you away, and that was all. . . ."

"That's what you thought?" Anne interrupted. "After ten years. Very impressive."

"Think so?" Terrier glanced at her, then looked back at the road. "What I had in mind was a rather primitive country, with a good climate, a weak currency, and easygoing relations between people."

"That sort of thing exists, then?" asked Anne. She seemed amused, sardonic.

"My preferences tended toward Ceylon," Terrier explained calmly. "Because in Africa or Latin America, it's over, it's completely ruined. Completely!" he repeated, nodding his head with conviction. "But a place like Ceylon or Mauritius, or even more remote places, that would be really quiet." He frowned. "But maybe they're going down the drain, too. There's the Tamils in Ceylon, and there's trouble every now and then. I don't know." He shook his head worriedly. "And there's tourism. It's the same thing. Maybe worse."

"A desert island is what you need," said Anne.

Terrier shrugged.

"An island where they don't even know about money." He grunted weirdly. "But right now there's a different problem. Either a desert island or the exact opposite. I mean a place where you can get lost in the crowd. I don't know," he said again. "I'm fucked up. I'll think about it. I'm going to lower the back of your seat so you can sleep."

"I'm not a bit sleepy," said Anne. "If you want to sleep, though, I could drive."

Terrier gave her a perplexed look, as if she had something strange that didn't fit into his perspective. They spoke little after that. Around two-thirty in the morning they pulled up to a refreshment area. They drank cups of coffee from a machine. On Terrier's orders, Anne had pulled a woolen cap over her head after piling her hair up. When they left, the young woman took three long swigs of cognac.

"I'm not thirsty, but I should still get some sleep," she explained. But she did not sleep.

The DS left the highway and entered the Paris ring road at the Porte d'Orléans at six-fifteen Sunday morning. Terrier and Anne took a room at an expensive hotel in the seventh arrondissement, not far from the Esplanade des Invalides, under the name of Monsieur and Madame Walter.

"Generally," said the clerk, "we ask our guests to provide us with a credit card when they have no luggage." He looked politely at Terrier.

From inside his jacket, Terrier produced a bundle of ten thousand francs, in five-hundred-franc bills.

"Can you deposit this in the safe?" he asked.

"The cashier doesn't arrive till nine," said the clerk.

"I don't have a credit card," said Terrier. "Do you want an advance?"

"Please! Please!" exclaimed the clerk. "You'll be shown to your room." He rang. "Excuse me, monsieur," he added. "You understand."

Terrier did not reply. They were shown to their room.

"Maybe you think we're going to fuck," said Anne, when the door was closed.

"Pardon?"

Anne repeated what she had said.

"No," said Terrier. "Rest." He picked up the telephone.

"Yes," murmured Anne in a hesitant tone. She stopped for a moment, then she began to move and went into the bathroom.

Terrier dialed a number: there was no answer. The man frowned. He finally hung up. From the bathroom came the sound of water vigorously filling the tub. Anne had closed the door, but Terrier didn't hear her lock it. He approached the door.

"I'm going out for an hour or two," he said. "Go to bed and get some sleep."

In the bar downstairs he quickly drank two double espressos. Taking the DS from the hotel parking lot, he slowly headed north. It was eight-fifteen, Sunday morning: the streets were not very lively. When Terrier spotted an open service station, he parked a short distance away, then walked back to the place and made some purchases. He got back behind the wheel, then rushed into a vast underground parking structure near the Opéra. He deliberately descended to the lowest level, where there were few vehicles and less risk of being disturbed by a new arrival. He put on his gloves. Using a rag, he did his best to wipe down the interior of the DS and part of its exterior, particularly the door handles and the adjoining areas. Then he detached the license plates. With a can of spray paint acquired a few minutes earlier, he covered the license plate areas with black, applying just one coat; it was insufficient but would dry quickly. He used the detached plates as masks so that the four sides of the rectangle would be rectilinear and clearly set off.

He was disturbed only once. A door slammed, and steps resounded. Terrier slipped behind the DS and squatted down. At the other end of the parking structure, a fat man in a blue overcoat and white scarf slid uncomfortably behind the wheel of a Volvo. He started up and left without bothering to let the engine warm up. Terrier stood up and lighted a cigarette. It was freezing cold. Great dirty ventilators rumbled in the distance.

Then, on the still-sticky black paint, the man applied the white numbers and letters he had bought at the service station. Finally, with the license plates under his leather coat, Terrier climbed back up into the open air.

It was raining a little. It was now nine o'clock, and the streets were more animated. In the side streets Parisians hurried to the grocery stores that had just opened; on the boulevards groups of Japanese tourists circulated enthusiastically. Terrier dumped his spray-paint can and spattered gloves in one metro wastebasket and the license plates in another. After a brief train journey, he reemerged into the daylight and walked some two kilometers, sometimes stopping before a shopwindow, sometimes retracing his steps, and finally reached Faulques's apartment.

The financial adviser did not respond to the doorbell. Terrier frowned. He went back out into the courtyard. The bedroom shutters were closed, but not those of the office. Terrier stuck his face against the glass. There were lights on in the bedroom. The office was empty and in its usual disorder, as far as one could tell through the filthy yellow curtain.

Terrier returned to the hallway. The building was dilapidated and badly maintained. There was almost half a centimeter of light between Faulques's door and its warped jamb. Terrier used several of the many accessories in his Swiss Army knife. After a few minutes, he succeeded in working the latch and pushing open the door.

"Faulques? It's Charles."

The apartment smelled like the garbage cans of a Chinese pastry shop. Terrier closed the door behind him and went into the bedroom. Faulques was hanging by a silk scarf attached to big hook set up high on the wall, just below the ceiling. Below

Faulques's shoes, which were soiled with streaks of dried shit, the nightstand was overturned. The financial adviser's face had turned black and so had his tongue, which sprang from between his teeth like the tongue in a decapitated calf's head. He was wearing a shirt and pants. He had been dead for about forty-eight hours.

It was stifling in the apartment; the heat had been turned up to the highest setting. There was a sealed envelope on the pillow on the unmade bed. Terrier returned to the office, went over to the kitchenette, and put on a pair of gloves. He dug into the heaps of papers on the desk and on the floor, found a pile of new envelopes. He took one, returned to the bedroom, and opened the letter that rested on the pillow:

"I killed myself out of cowardice," said the typewritten message. "I used the money of certain clients for personal speculation. I gambled and I lost. I don't have the courage to face up to my responsibilities. Farewell to all, forgive me." There was a handwritten signature.

Terrier tossed what he was holding onto the pillow and abruptly sat down on the edge of the bed, crossing his gloved hands over his stomach. He leaned forward and gave a long sigh. His mouth was open, and he blinked repeatedly. He seemed to calm down after a moment. He got back up. Without looking at the hanged corpse, he refolded the message and slipped it into the new envelope that he had brought from the other room. He sealed the envelope and placed it on the pillow. He crumpled the used envelope and tossed it into the overflowing wastebasket near the desk. Retracing his steps through the communicating door, he briefly studied Faulques's body, then he went out and pulled the door shut behind him.

13

With his collar turned up, Terrier stepped out onto Rue de la Victoire and headed for the closest metro station without breaking his stride.

A few meters along, he crossed the street, glancing mechanically first to the left then to the right, without slowing down. People were waiting in line in front of a bakery. A guy was reading *Le Monde diplomatique* in a parked Peugeot 404; he seemed to be waiting for someone, probably his wife out shopping. A young girl in a print housecoat had just opened the shutters of a second-floor window right across from Faulques's. She closed the window again and briskly drew the curtains. Emerging from a delicatessen, a mom slapped the brat she had in tow, and he started howling. Terrier hurried on.

A few minutes later, he found a taxi and asked to be taken to Place de la Nation.

During the journey, he noticed that a 404 was following them, keeping a substantial distance between itself and the taxi. Just after turning a corner, with the 404 out of sight for an instant, Terrier took Faulques's gloves, which he had kept till now, and threw them out the open window.

"What did you throw out? You threw something out, didn't you?" asked the driver. He didn't seem too sure.

"Some wrapping paper," said Terrier.

"A little filth makes Paris beautiful," the driver declared sententiously, and then he burst into a gigantic laugh before calming down and adding that Paris was nothing but an enormous piece of shit, in any case. "As for me, I'm working for three more years and then I'm out of here. I have a little house near La Ferté-sous-Jouarre, and I'm out of here, what you'd call gone!" He heaved a sigh of anger. "To live a little. . . . Shit, I'm not going to wait till World War III to get a life. Tomorrow it will be too late!"

Since the man was the talkative type, Terrier uttered a few approving grunts and favorable exclamations during the journey, and the driver ranted and raved nonstop. According to him, the world was going to remain pretty much the same for five, maybe six years, except for noticeable worsening in some areas, but that was nothing compared with the fact that everything was really going to blow up later on.

"The Pakistanis, the Hindus, the Iranians, and all the rest won't have to drop bombs on us," the man explained. "They'll come quietly on foot. We'll never be able to kill them all. They'll just swallow us up. Say, did you screw someone's wife?"

"Excuse me?"

The driver repeated the question. "Because a 404 has been on our tail for a while." They were arriving at Place de la Nation.

"A coincidence."

"Wouldn't you like me to take a spin around the Place to make sure?"

"No, thanks," said Terrier, laughing. "You read too many crime novels. And I'm in a hurry."

The driver shrugged and came to a stop. Terrier paid him off and went into the Printemps-Nation store, where he bought several items, including a suitcase. Leaving the department store with his other purchases in the suitcase, he crossed Place de la Nation at a good clip. At the Canon de la Nation café, he ordered a small beer at the counter, then went downstairs to telephone.

"Where are you?" asked Stanley.

Terrier didn't answer. He asked the black man if he had been able to find out anything about the subject they had spoken of earlier.

"No," said Stanley. "I'm sorry."

"Then can you say something about the general atmosphere?"

"Hard to say. Nervous, I would say. Yes, nervous."

"Really?"

"They're getting ready for a job," said Stanley. "That's what it seems like to me. It's only an impression, mind you. I don't share the secrets of the powers that be, you know. At the moment, I hardly do anything more than handle the mail." Stanley worked for UNESCO; he traveled to unlikely places like Turkestan or the Philippines. "I can't really ask questions. I can only sniff the air. There's a big job in preparation."

"Nothing about me?"

"Nothing."

"If necessary," asked Terrier, "can you put someone up for a little while? In your Fontainebleau place?"

"My Larchant place, you mean. Who? You? Of course. As long as you like."

"I don't know yet," said Terrier. "We'll see. I'll call back." Through the door of the booth he was watching to see if anyone came down to piss or anything.

"You can count on me, in any case," said Stanley. "You know that."

"Of course. Thank you." Terrier hung up.

He went back upstairs and slowly drank his beer at the counter. From the other side of the avenue a passerby was passing by, a copy of *Le Monde diplomatique* folded in four in his pocket. Terrier paid up, then headed toward the metro entrance on Place de la Nation with his suitcase. As soon as he was below ground, he began to run.

He caught a moving train. At the Châtelet station, he made a series of zigzags. In a recess, some Scandinavians were playing an excruciating arrangement of *Death and the Maiden* for flute, harmonica, and violin. In a corridor, six rockers were beating up another rocker and stealing his boots.

After a complicated journey, Terrier reached his hotel around noon. At a counter he bought *Le Journal du Dimanche*. The room was empty. On the nightstand, the radio played quietly. Anne had left a note on the bedspread to say: "I'm going for a walk." Terrier tightened his lips a little, and they went slightly pale. He sat down on the edge of the bed. He suddenly appeared very tired. He rubbed his shoulders and other joints. He fiddled with the radio. A long-wave newscaster recited "the news headlines." The sudden death of a Chinese government official, the saber rattling of a Persian Gulf potentate named Sheik Hakim, the position of the French in an international ski competition, and the popularity ratings of leading politicians in a recent opinion poll—that was about it. Terrier turned down the radio, stretched out on the bed, and unfolded the newspaper. An article was titled "Massacre at the Beach." Terrier read it quickly. It recounted, with a few details, the death of Félix Schrader and three unknown persons, including a woman, and the disappearance of Anne Schrader: that's all there was. Terrier crumpled up the newspaper and threw it on the floor. He closed his eyes and breathed deeply and regularly. He seemed to doze for a while. Then his eyes opened again. He made a pout, looked at his watch, and made a pout again. He got out of bed, put the "Ne pas déranger—Do Not Disturb" sign on the door, locked up, pulled the thick double curtains, took the weapons he had collected, and laid them out on the bed.

Since the double curtains allowed a little light to filter through, the man covered his eyes with his tie. Working blindly and by touch, during the course of half an hour he disassembled and reassembled the Colt Special Agent, the CZ, and the Savage. He was very fast. He would have been even faster if his little finger had not been hurt.

And then, after putting away the weapons and opening the curtains, he went into the bathroom with his suitcase. He showered, shaved, and changed clothes, putting on a cheap, new iron-gray suit over a dark gray shirt. Coming out of the bathroom, he checked his watch again (it was one-thirty) and picked up the telephone. He remained motionless for a moment, the receiver held away from his face as he listened to the dial tone; his features expressed nothing, or else they expressed deep disturbance. Then he dialed a number. Even though it was Sunday, and lunchtime, he reached someone at the other end. Without the slightest hesitation, he dictated the text of a classified ad so that it would be typeset in advance and space reserved, and he promised to stop by to pay before five o'clock.

He had a plate of cold cuts and German beer sent up, which he consumed as he listened to the radio. For a time, he stopped chewing while, between a bit of jazz and a ditty, the set played a song by Purcell for countertenor entitled, as Terrier knew, "O Lead Me to Some Peaceful Gloom." However, with an impatient gesture, as if he were angry at losing his concentration, he began chewing again well before the end of the song. When he had finished eating, he composed a brief message for Anne: "I'll be gone till three o'clock. Don't go out again. Don't write any checks." He underscored the last sentence three times.

He had placed the message on the bed and slipped on his leather coat and was heading toward the door when the young woman came in with a smile.

"Where were you, for Christ's sake?" asked Terrier.

"I was taking a walk. You didn't find my note?"

Terrier nodded. Intuitively, Anne looked at the bedspread, where she had left her message and where Terrier's now lay. She picked it up and skimmed through it. She turned toward Terrier.

"Of course I wouldn't write any checks. Do you take me for an idiot?"

"Anne," said Terrier, "perhaps it would be better if you went to the cops. You can say that I took you hostage and brought you here to Paris."

"So you're starting that again?" she cried.

"Anne," Terrier repeated. "Anne." His lips moved, but he no longer seemed capable of speaking. "I'm ruined," he said suddenly.

"What?" It was a question, but at the same time it was a nervous laugh.

"I'm ruined," Terrier repeated. He seemed immensely serious. "I believe all my money's been lost. I can't explain it, but it's lost. I don't believe that I'll be able to get it back. So I have to work again. Don't laugh!" he shouted, because she was laughing, laughing in his face. "I have to work!" he repeated violently. "I must do my job!"

Anne twirled around the room, then sat down on the edge of the bed and looked at the man. She was no longer laughing, but she was still smiling.

"Ah," she said. "Your job. Bang-bang again."

"You're insane," said Terrier.

"Go on now!" Anne exclaimed. "I'll wait for you. I'm beat. I'm going to sleep a little."

"You should go to the cops. It's better."

"We'll see," said Anne.

For an instant, Terrier seemed to want to talk some more, then he gave up and turned away. He left the room. Laughing, Anne lay down on the bedspread, then she cried, then she became very calm and tired, then she fell asleep, all within three minutes. Terrier had left the hotel and was walking toward the metro. At times, his lips moved. But he made no sound. Knitting his brow, he took the train and went to the main office of *Le Monde,* where he paid in cash for the ad that he had earlier dictated without hesitation on the telephone. The text would appear in the next day's public announcements section under the heading, "Movers: "Christian A. Cox, house clearance specialist, open for business after renovation"—followed by the telephone number of the hotel and the words: "Ask for Monsieur Walter."

14

"Well, it was only dislocated," said the doctor on duty, whose address Terrier had found on a list in the window of a closed pharmacy. "You straightened it out yourself? Seriously?"

"Yes."

"Bravo. You're a pretty stoic fellow."

According to the doctor, there was no call to put it in a cast. He showed Terrier how to use an elastic bandage so that the swollen finger would stay completely immobilized.

"I know," said Terrier.

He left with his X-ray and a prescription for an anti-inflammatory cream and some painkillers; he threw the X-ray into a sewer opening, bought the medicine in an on-duty pharmacy, and returned to the hotel via the metro. Anne was sleeping. She was crying in her sleep. Terrier studied her. He had an anxious, perplexed expression. Since the young woman continued to moan in a miserable, infantile way, he took her by the shoulders. She was naked in the bed. He gently shook her. She opened her eyes and stared at him with a lost look, then she rubbed her eyes with her fists, stared at him again, and smiled mischievously.

"Bedtime," she said. "Get into bed."

Terrier spotted a half-empty bottle of Hennessy cognac between the bed and the wall. Anne's speech was slurred. The man straightened up and turned his back on her.

"Try to listen carefully," he ordered. "We're going to have to separate temporarily. By tomorrow afternoon, my employers will know that they can find me here. I would rather keep you out of all this."

"Keep me out of it?" Anne repeated. "That's a good one!"

"Seriously."

"I'm a big girl, you know."

"Yes, I know. But if they know where you are, that gives them a way to pressure me."

"Oh," Anne said disdainfully. "And where am I supposed to go?"

"Near Larchant. It's south of the Fontainebleau forest. I have a friend who has a house there. I believe I can count on him."

"You're well organized."

"Unfortunately not." Terrier glanced at Anne over his shoulder. "You'll have to remain on your own for quite a while. But a friend spends his weekends there. You don't have anything against blacks?"

"What?"

Anne seemed dumbfounded. Terrier repeated the question.

"Because that's what he is," he explained. "My pal is black."

"But what do you take me for?"

"I don't know. I know very little about you," Terrier said softly.

"Come to bed."

"I don't know." Terrier's tone was indecisive at first, then firmed up. "First, we have to take care of practicalities."

Anne sat up in bed, exposing her breasts, which were still beautiful, though heavy and just beginning to sag. She grabbed the bottle of cognac.

"How many people have you killed?"

"Don't drink any more! We have to take care of practicalities! Practicalities!" Terrier repeated nervously. With his hands in his pockets, he was facing Anne and rocking impatiently on his heels. The young woman took a swig from the bottle.

"You're on the blink," she declared in a neutral tone. She might as well have been pronouncing a diagnosis concerning a broken clock. "On the blink. Come to bed, then." She threw herself violently back down, with her eyes hermetically sealed, without letting go of the bottle. Her whole face was red, and a flush spread across her throat and breasts. "Let's fuck." She opened her eyes. "That's what you wanted," she said decisively.

"Shit, Anne, wait a second!" Terrier shouted uselessly. The door of the room, which Terrier had neglected to lock, opened behind him, and two guys came in. One of them quietly closed the door, and the other put the barrel of an S&W Bodyguard Airweight revolver to Terrier's head.

"The company sent us," explained the man with the revolver. "Don't do anything stupid."

"Anne, stay calm," said Terrier.

"Who are these faggots?" asked the young woman. She was still flat on her back, bare-breasted, red-faced, bottle in hand.

Without moving his head, Terrier turned his eyes toward the weaponless man as he was crossing the room. It was the short guy with black eyes that Terrier had already seen on the balcony in the apartment in Rue de Varenne; he was wearing the same gray overcoat.

"If you knock me off," said Terrier, "compromising information will be made known to the public."

"No one's getting knocked off. We've come to fetch you. Who's the naked lady?"

"You can let her go," said Terrier. "She won't say anything."

"Anne Schrader, huh? Get dressed."

"Quick work," said Terrier.

"I'm not going to repeat it a hundred times," the short guy cautioned Anne.

Anne put the bottle down, threw back the bedclothes, and began dressing with swift motions.

"Nice ass," the short guy commented. "A beautiful woman." He turned back to Terrier. "My compliments." He searched Terrier, then the room; he pocketed the weapons. "We're going downstairs. You'll pay the bill. Here's some cash." He stuffed a wad into Terrier's pocket. "A car is waiting for us. If you screw around, my friend here will blow your head off, and I'll plug your whore in the belly. Got it?"

Terrier nodded. The short guy picked up their stuff and put it under his arm. Anne had finished dressing, so they got going. Terrier could see the face of the man with the revolver. He had seen him before: a copy of *Le Monde diplomatique* folded in four was still sticking out of his pocket.

Downstairs, Anne and the man with the revolver stayed in the middle of the lobby while the short guy accompanied Terrier to the reception desk, where the bill was drawn up and paid. The HK4, the Savage, the CZ, and the Colt Special Agent caused the pockets of the gray overcoat to bulge. They went out into the glacial night. A Renault 16 was waiting, a mixed-race Indochinese man at the wheel. Terrier sat next to the driver while the other two flanked Anne in the back. The Renault crossed the Seine and headed toward Saint-Augustin. The roads were oily and slippery, vaguely reflecting the illuminated signs, the lighted shopwindows, and the headlights and taillights of moving vehicles. There was a risk of ice forming in the coming hours.

"Listen, Christian," the short guy said to Martin Terrier. "I hope there's no misunderstanding. We're bringing you to see Cox. We didn't take any chances, and that's normal. But it's all nice and friendly—don't think otherwise."

"Okay."

They parked in Rue La Boétie and went into an office building, where they took a broken-down elevator. Without knocking, they went through a door bearing a sign that read "IMPEX FILMS INTERNATIONAL."

"There's an annex of the Ministry of the Interior across the way," said the short guy as he smiled and pointed a finger at the windowpanes, which were opaque with filth. "The day you want to raise the level of tension in France, just take a bazooka and boom!" He laughed.

Terrier and Anne stood waiting in the empty office with the man with the revolver and the Eurasian driver. The short guy had slipped out through a communicating door. He reappeared and signaled to Terrier.

"Come in. The girl stays here."

"If something goes wrong, shout," Terrier said to Anne.

He went into the next room. Seated at a metal desk, Cox was eating fries with his fingers from a paper plate. He was wearing a gray flannel three-piece suit and hadn't taken off his camel's hair overcoat, which was hanging open around him. He had a spot of grease on his double chin. He seemed tired.

"Would you like some coffee?" he asked. "There's a coffee maker. Would you like some fries? I don't have anything else to offer you." Martin shook his head. "I'm glad you changed your mind," Cox said, affecting great conviction.

"You've read my ad already?"

"Of course."

"In tomorrow's paper?"

"Of course," Cox repeated. "We don't use a hundred different press outlets for our correspondence. It's not hard to pay the odd employee for advance knowledge of a small section of the classified ads. Pure routine, Christian." He smiled. "Martin Terrier, I should say."

"Did you know that from the beginning?"

"We like to be well acquainted with our employees. You've screwed things up in a big way." Cox was still smiling. "You have this Anne Schrader with you, it seems."

Terrier nodded. Cox shrugged.

"Is it important to you? Does she matter to you?" Terrier didn't answer. Cox smiled at him again. "Are we still in agreement on one hundred and fifty thousand francs?"

"Two hundred thousand," said Terrier. "You talked about two hundred thousand."

"That was before you were run to ground. Now it's one hundred and fifty, and that's still a good price. And there are some in-kind benefits: you and this woman, papers, passports, all the necessaries. The target in two weeks. Until then, you'll be taken care of, naturally."

"I don't want the girl taken care of. I want you to let her go."

"Of course that's what you want," said Cox. "It's impossible, of course." He glanced wearily at Terrier. "Do you want to argue? Do you want to waste our time?"

"No. Where will the target be?"

"Here. In Paris."

"I want to spend the two-week wait in the South Sea Islands," said Terrier.

"Why?" asked Cox with genuine surprise.

"Because I can't think of anything better. Where would you go, in my position?"

"I wouldn't budge."

"That's not surprising."

"You're stupid, Christian," said Cox with a kind of anger. "You're an idiot. I wouldn't make a move from here or any other place where I happened to be, because there's not one place that's any different from any other anymore, except for the communist countries, which are even worse. There's no place good anymore, don't you understand? No, I wouldn't budge! There's nowhere to go."

"I want to go to the South Sea Islands," Terrier said again.

"You will go to the Tronçais forest," Cox said firmly.

15

It was an old country house that had been transformed into a sort of hunting lodge. The ground floor consisted of three rooms: a common room that doubled as a kitchen, with stone sinks, a cast-iron stove, and a big table covered with an oil-cloth; a bedroom; and, finally, a small room with an uneven tile floor that was part storeroom and part living room, with its logs and armchairs, its hearth and little stone table, and its rifles in a display case. Beneath the tile roof, the attic had been converted into an immense studio whose walls were paneled in varnished fir. There was an ornamental garden enclosed by a low stone wall with suburban-style iron railings on top; the building was situated in the forest, eight hundred meters from a main road across the Allier département. Anne Schrader and Martin Terrier had been brought there in a horse van the night after Terrier and Cox's meeting.

The short guy in the gray overcoat and his *Le Monde diplomatique*–reading acolyte had spelled each other at the wheel. They had arrived around three o'clock in the morning. Three flashes of the headlights had quickly roused the caretakers of the place. Anne and Terrier had been taken upstairs via an interior staircase that was steep and simple like a ladder. The drivers had departed again almost immediately.

"I was just coming to fetch you," the caretaker said when Terrier left the converted attic by a trap door and descended the staircase around ten-thirty on the morning of the eleventh day.

The caretaker called himself Maubert. He must have been a few years older than Terrier—perhaps thirty-five. He was big and muscular, with a thick head of blond hair parted on the side and a thick blond mustache on a narrow face with a long, thin nose. His eyes were slightly slanted and a little too close together. The skin of his face and hands was tanned and weather-beaten. He always wore wide-wale corduroy trousers and plaid flannel shirts. He looked like an advertisement for American cigarettes. When he went out, he would put on rubber boots and a lumber jacket, but right now he was in shirtsleeves and carpet slippers. Once Terrier was down, Maubert beckoned him into the combination living room and storeroom. The caretaker's girlfriend was cooking something in a pot on the stove and didn't turn around as Terrier went by.

A log fire made a low roar in the fireplace. The house dog, a setter, wasn't there; it must have been roving in the forest. On the surface of the stone table were blue chalk marks, some toy motorcycle police, and three miniature cars: two Citroën SMs and one Citroën Pallas.

"Let's sit down," said Maubert. "Beer? Coffee? Something else?"

"No."

They sat down on rustic wooden chairs with cushions. Maubert picked up a miniature Renault van from the uneven tile floor and kept it in his hands, passing it from one palm to the other. Terrier, leaning forward, examined the miniature cars and motorcycle cops. They were not to the same scale. Still, this was clearly a convoy. And the chalk marks were the street plan.

"Here is the Champs-Elysées roundabout," said Maubert, putting his index finger on the stone table top. "North is that way. So this is the beginning of the Champs-Elysées, which doesn't interest us. And this is Avenue Montaigne." He pointed to Avenue Montaigne, which was shown in its entirety, from the Champs-Elysées roundabout to Place de l'Alma; the miniature vehicles were positioned on Avenue Montaigne. "Are you familiar with this part of Paris?"

"Yes."

"Then you know that it's a one-way avenue with a service road on either side, both running in the same direction as the avenue." He put the Renault van on the edge of the avenue. "You will be inside this, stationed in the left-hand service road, just short of the junction with Rue Bayard." He looked at Terrier as if expecting him to say something, but Terrier said nothing. "I will be your driver." Terrier sat up slightly and contemplated Maubert, but he made no comment and turned back to the crude map and the models. "The back of our vehicle," continued Maubert, "consists of a hatchback for the top half and two doors for the bottom half. The target will come down the avenue. You can choose the position and the field of fire as you please. You can have one door open or two, if you fire from the prone position; or you can have the hatchback open, if you want to fire from a standing position and lean on the closed doors. You can have all three open, if you want, but I don't see the point in that."

With his elbows on his knees, Terrier leaned forward and dangled a hand over the miniature convoy. With two fingers, he described a vague circle.

"Where is the target?"

"In the back of the Pallas. Four motorcycle cops will lead the way, followed by an SM, then the Pallas, with the second SM behind, just as they are here."

"It's suicide," said Terrier.

"No."

"Yes, it is." Terrier sat back in his rustic armchair and shook his head. He sniggered disdainfully. "The four motorcycle cops aside, there will be cops in the cars. They will be on us in a flash. If we try to get away, they'll turn us into confetti. It's completely ridiculous. It's suicide."

"No, not at all," Maubert said again, smiling. "I belong to the Direction de la Surveillance du Territoire." Terrier raised an eyebrow. "We won't even try to get away," said the blond man. "There's a false sheet-metal floor. You'll lie down and close the false floor over you, and the van stays put. I'll get out and identify myself. After all, I really have been ordered to mount surveillance on the target."

"Who is it?"

"An OPEC camel jockey, Sheik Hakim. Does that mean anything to you?"

"I must have seen him on TV."

"Yeah, me too," Maubert said distractedly. He smiled again. "My superiors really have charged me with keeping him under surveillance. I have written orders. And there will be a diversion." He looked at Terrier with a smile, again seeming to expect comments that never came. "There's a guy who will be on the top floor of a building on the other side of the avenue: he will spray the convoy with machine-gun fire. He'll be given tracer bullets. He may have just enough time to go down and get out to Rue de Marignan through the cellars. He believes he will, in any case. I'd be surprised if he makes it. On the other hand, the cops are such idiots."

"Is your man named Oswald?" asked Terrier.

"Very funny," said Maubert. He wasn't smiling at all now. "Do you have an idea of what weapon you'll use?"

"I'm thinking." Terrier closed his eyes. "I need a rapid-fire automatic assault rifle. One that will take a silencer."

"An Ingram," suggested Maubert.

"I don't think so. I'd prefer something else. I think I'd like bullets that travel faster than sound, so that the shots seem to come from the other side of the avenue."

"I don't know if we can have that for you in three days." Maubert puffed out his cheeks and grimaced. "In any case, the silencer will slow it down."

"Failing that," said Terrier, "get me something simple and solid—a Weatherby or something like that. I would also like a revolver."

"That's not part of the plan."

"If things go wrong," said Terrier, "I'd rather have a revolver." He looked at Maubert candidly. During the past ten days, the caretaker had shown himself to be helpful and efficient. He had quickly and correctly satisfied all of Anne and Terrier's requests in regard to clothing, food, cigarettes, beverages, and other needs. He had even provided Terrier with a compact hi-fi system and a stack of records, for which he must have had to go to Montluçon or Moulins. Only the walks taken by the two guests were subject to pronounced constraints. "I would like a large-caliber revolver with a short barrel," added Terrier.

"I'll see if that's possible."

Terrier bent forward again to study the convoy on the stone table.

"It will be at night, I suppose."

"The camel jockey will eat at the Elysée Palace. Usually, there's an hour and a half of talk with the president after chowing down; the ladies get to listen to chamber music. Usually, the convoy leaves the palace at twelve-thirty in the morning."

"The later the better," said Terrier. "Because of the movie theaters letting out and all. So that the streets are clear." He shook his head, stood up, and looked at his watch. "I'd like to take a little walk before lunch and think it over."

Maubert stood up, too. He gave Terrier a tense look. Terrier smiled at him. Maubert's cheek twitched. He half-opened the communicating door.

"Cécile!" he called. "Monsieur Christian wants to take a walk."

A minute or two later, Terrier and Cécile were walking quickly in the biting cold on one of the rudely surfaced straight trails through the Tronçais forest and which the local people call "lines." On either side of the path clusters of tall oaks and other broad-leaved trees, bare in this season, alternated with young thickets and zones of clear-cutting. At scattered intervals, the environmental agency had painted its symbol on the bark of particular trees. Here and there limbed and bucked logs lay alongside the line. Beneath the thickets, on the thick layer of decomposing leaves, lay remnants of last week's snowfall. Mist hung in the hollows, over the wallows, and over the streams bordered by ice. The air was damp and, because of the direction of the wind that whistled through the bare branches, one could not even hear the engines of the rare vehicles that slipped down the highway, two or three kilometers away.

Before leaving on the walk, Terrier had gone upstairs to tell Anne that he was going out. Naked and disheveled on one of the two beds, the young woman was warming a snifter half full of cognac between her palms. She had smiled mechanically.

"On the blink," she had said. "Impotent. Go freeze them off, then."

"I've told you already," Terrier had said. "It's because I'm on a job. It's my concentration." He had nodded with conviction. "That's it. That's all it is."

At present, Terrier was striding along behind Cécile, observing her. Maubert's companion had long bleached hair that floated down her back; it was not very clean, and the dark roots showed. She was tall and obviously thin despite the layered sweaters under her anorak—a plebian skinniness. Arriving at one of the star-shaped crossroads that the local people call "circles," she came to a stop and turned around to face Terrier. She indicated a line that made an acute angle with the one they had just walked down.

"Shall we go back this way?" she asked. She looked bored.

"I want to go a little farther," said Terrier.

"Out of the question. Verboten. How many times do I have to say it?"

"Are you sure?" Terrier slipped the fingers of his right hand between the girl's hair and her neck and caressed her under the chin with his thumb.

"Hey," she said with a smile, without moving. "Hands off!"

Terrier put his left hand on the other side of the girl's neck. He knew exactly where to press with his thumbs, and that's where he pressed. She frowned, then raised her eyebrows and opened her mouth. Terrier pulled her close and blocked her arms with his elbows. His right leg parried the knee that the girl tried to jam in his parts. Seconds later, Cécile did not even have the strength to keep her eyes open, and her lower jaw hung slack. She would soon have been dead if Terrier had not relaxed the pressure, but he did relax the pressure. The setter, which had been gamboling out in front of the walkers for the last quarter of an hour, had now come and planted itself next to the pair. Its bark was worried and threatening. Terrier took the dog's leash from Cécile's pocket and allowed the unconscious girl to slip to the ground. The dog stopped barking and attacked very fast. Terrier coolly buried his left fist in its open muzzle; with his right hand he seized the animal by its collar. As he immobilized the dog, which was trying to fight back as it noisily strangled, the man worked the clasp of the leash. Then he pulled his fist out of the muzzle, the dog's fangs scraping his hand as he did so.

Three minutes later, the unconscious Cécile was seated against the trunk of an isolated Norwegian fir, whose lower branches hung down and hid her from hypothetical passersby. She would regain consciousness in a few minutes. She risked catching a bad cold, even though Terrier had scrupulously put her hands in her pockets after wrapping her head in her scarf. Attached to a branch by its leash, the setter was now calm, licking the girl's face and whining now and then.

Meanwhile, Terrier was running powerfully and steadily down a line in the direction that had always been forbidden on his walks. And almost immediately he reached the edge of the forest and came out on a secondary road. A hundred meters farther on was a village with six or seven stoplights, a bus stop, and a bar and general store that had a news rack. The man went into the shop, mechanically rubbing his left hand, which still had the setter's dried saliva on it, against his thigh. He ordered a muscadet and asked for the telephone. There was a telephone booth. Once more Terrier told Stanley what he thought it judicious to tell him—and asked him for what it seemed possible to ask.

"No problem," said Stanley.

"Forgive me for not telling you everything," said Terrier.

"It's less dangerous for you if I don't explain everything."

"Okay," said Stanley, rather primly.

"Stanley," Terrier said abruptly, "my name isn't Christian. Did you know that?"

"What's this all about?"

"Did you know that?"

"No."

"See you soon," Terrier said as he hung up.

He paid and left the store. He went back into the forest and, at a run, cut straight through the woods to the house. He soundlessly entered the deserted common room, soundlessly ascended the steep staircase, and soundlessly edged his way into the interior of the converted attic, where he saw that Anne was straddling Maubert, who was stretched out on his back, and fucking him.

16

Terrier's face turned pink, except for the edges of his lips, which turned pale. Unfaithful once more, his companion had her back to him. Terrier could see Maubert's legs, his trousers still on. The copulating couple had not heard the man come into the converted attic because a record player was loudly playing Verdi. The monks of *Il Trovatore* were chanting:

Miserere d'un'alma già vicina
alla partenza che non ha ritorno.
Miserere di lei, bontà divina,
preda non sia dell'infernal soggiorno.

. . . And simultaneously, Leonora (Leontyne Price, a magnificent black beauty) was singing:

Sull'orrida torre,
ahi! par che la morte
con ali di tenebre
librando si va!
Ahi! forse dischiuse
gli fian queste porte
sol quando cadaver
già freddo sarà!

. . . and so forth. Terrier moved his lips several times and several times uttered a low sound like a sigh, and his face reverted to a homogeneous pallor. He finally went and stopped the record player by pulling out the plug. The opera slowed and groaned to a stop. In the silence, the setter could be heard barking some distance away outside. Anne had jumped to her feet next to the bed. Hands on hips, she looked Terrier up and down and seemed shocked, even offended and furious. Maubert had sat up. Without looking at anyone, he struggled to put his swollen dick back into his briefs; then he stood up to close the zipper of his trousers. Finally, he met Terrier's gaze. From downstairs came the sounds of the setter and Cécile rushing agitatedly back into the house. Cécile yelled for Maubert.

"Go downstairs," Anne told him.

"Cécile could care less," said Maubert. "We're not together."

"Go downstairs."

Maubert headed for the trap door that led downstairs. He had to pass very close to Terrier, who was standing motionless with his fingers rigidly extended. The professional killer breathed slowly. Maubert gave him an uncertain glance.

"Let me by. Don't do anything stupid."

Terrier nodded. Maubert went past and disappeared through the trap door. Terrier went and sat on the corner of the bed. Anne had wiped her crotch with a handful of Kleenex and was quickly getting dressed.

"Idiot!" she said. "So what did you expect?" Seemingly calm, Terrier paid her close attention. "Idiot!" Anne repeated. "Just tell me, what did you think? Did you think I was going to wait ten years? Do you think I'm going to wait ten more years? Do you think there was only Félix, before? Do you take me for some brainless little porcelain doll? What do you take me for? I'm sick and tired of this. Cretin! Fag!" Terrier shrugged. Anne sat down heavily at the head of the bed and eyed him. "I cheated on Félix. So what do you expect?"

An indistinct sound came from Terrier's throat. Anne watched him; she frowned. The man made vague gestures. He got up, looked around for something, turned back to Anne, and pretended to write in his palm.

"What is it?" asked Anne. "Don't tell me you think the room is bugged!"

Terrier was insistent. Anne rummaged through her things and produced a small notebook with a tiny pencil. Terrier wrote carefully. Downstairs, Maubert and Cécile were having a vociferous argument. Terrier handed the open notebook to Anne. She read it and looked at Terrier with arched eyebrows. Since he did not seem to be joking, she reread it.

"You've got to be kidding!"

Terrier smiled and shook his head. He had painstakingly written: "I can't speak anymore. Complete aphonia. I think it's because of the psychological shock. But I don't understand it."

Anne looked Terrier quickly up and down as if there was something strange about him. There was actually something strange about him. She half smiled, as though this strangeness interested her, perhaps even agreeably disturbed her. Then she became hard again, even sarcastic.

"Stop playing the fool. Seriously, what's going on? Are you mute?" Terrier nodded. "You really can't talk?" He nodded again. She seemed about to burst out laughing or else get very angry. "Because of me?" she asked. "Ha! That's a good one—that takes the cake!" She shook her head. "But you must be kidding. It can't be true."

Terrier nodded once again. He picked up the notebook and wrote: "I'm not kidding. I'm fucked up. I'm sure it will go away. Right now, I have important things to tell you. You must obey me to the letter." He tore off the page and handed it to Anne. As she was reading, he wrote at top speed. When she finished reading, she watched him write. She seemed mystified but interested. He yanked off another page and gave it to her. Just then, Maubert and Cécile burst through the trap door. Maubert was waving a rifle. Cécile was disheveled and furious. Terrier scribbled something and handed it to Maubert, who hesitated before taking the piece of paper.

"He can't talk," said Anne.

"Up to here with both of you," read the piece of paper that Maubert was holding. "Neutralized Cécile to remind you I'm dangerous. Took a quiet little walk, that's all."

"You've lost your voice?"

Terrier nodded.

"He can't talk," Anne repeated.

"From now on, I'll communicate in writing," wrote Terrier. He tore off another page and held out the piece of paper.

"You're nuts. You're really nuts, pal," said Maubert.

"It's an attack of nerves," said Anne.

"Now leave me the fuck alone," Terrier declared in writing.

Maubert looked at Terrier, who gave him a half-smile and held out the notebook. Maubert shook his head.

"It's a trick," he said. Terrier shrugged. "Let's eat while I think it over."

No one said much during the meal, and Terrier didn't say anything at all. Cécile shot him hostile glances, but she didn't try to argue with him because Maubert had explained the situation to her. Maubert seemed to be thinking as he ate mouthfuls of stew. Looking vacant, Anne picked at her food. Terrier ate heartily.

"I'll bring the bosses up to date—that's the best thing," said Maubert at the end of the meal. He went toward the telephone, coffee cup in hand.

Anne and Terrier went upstairs. Terrier immediately began writing in the notebook. He showed Anne what he had written. She read it and looked at him with a doubtful expression. Terrier nodded emphatically.

"Yes," said Anne. "That makes sense."

She sighed and got up from the bed. Half an hour later, when Maubert knocked on the trap door and came in, he saw that the roofing in one area had been destroyed. The ceiling laths had been loosened and pulled out, the tar paper had been broken through and the layer of fiber-glass insulation pulled out; finally, tiles had been carefully taken down so as to make an opening in the roof. The winter air now poured in through this opening, making it cold in the converted attic. Maubert shivered. Terrier was stretched out on the bed, leafing through an old issue of *Le Chasseur français*. Anne had disappeared.

"Where has she gotten to, for Christ's sake?" Maubert asked hopelessly.

Terrier handed him a bit of paper on which he had neatly written: "I have removed Anne because with her held captive the bosses had a hold over me. She's in a safe place. The operation will continue as planned." Maubert sighed and sat down on the end of the bed. He looked distractedly at the gaping roof.

"You've got me in deep shit now," he said. "I suppose I'd better call the bosses again."

He stayed a moment where he was, looking morose and pensive, then went down to telephone. He came back up a quarter of an hour later, rubbing his hands together in a mechanical, reflective way.

"We'll continue as planned," he said. "There's nothing else we can do. I want no more of your tricks, though."

Terrier smiled vaguely. He spent the next two days reading

old magazines and, every now and then, smoking. It was pleasant in the attic: Maubert had patched the hole in the roof. Terrier would go downstairs for meals.

"You still can't talk?" Maubert would ask him every now and then, trying to salve his conscience. Terrier shook his head.

Cécile served the food with brusque gestures. She never looked Terrier in the eye.

"Get your things ready," Maubert said to Terrier at the end of one dinner. "We're leaving for Paris within the hour."

Terrier nodded as he continued to pour himself coffee. Later, the two men came out of the country house. A royal blue Estafette van was parked in front of the building; since when, Terrier didn't know.

"Hey! Hold on!" shouted Cécile from the front door.

She signaled for Terrier to come back. She gave him a kiss as cold and wet as a raw clam. She gave him an icy look.

"Go get yourself killed," she said.

Maubert was behind the wheel of the Estafette. Terrier got in beside him. The van turned into the road and drove off into the night.

17

To get back to Paris, they headed toward Orléans, where they got on Autoroute A10. It was cold but dry. The little van went fast.

"You can take a look at the materiel in back," said Maubert some ten minutes after their departure. He gestured toward a diver's flashlight, covered in black rubber, in the glove compartment.

Terrier took the light into the back of the vehicle. He began by examining the false floor of the van. The depth of the hiding place was very restricted. The man didn't try to lay down in it. He then opened a long, narrow case that resembled a large saxophone case. It contained the parts of a Finnish-made Valmet assault rifle, a telescopic sight, and a Lyman scope. Terrier assembled and disassembled the weapon, except for the scopes. He carefully examined the parts and the mechanism of the Valmet, which was unfamiliar to him. He put everything away and returned to the cab, where Maubert had turned on the radio and was listening to Radio Luxembourg. The driver glanced at Terrier, who grimaced discontentedly.

"You'll have three thirty-shot magazines," said Maubert. "You'll get them in due course. That should be enough, right?" He half smiled. "7.62mm," he added. Terrier nodded slightly and tapped an ear with his middle finger. "Don't worry," said Maubert. "With the other shooter letting loose with tracers, no one's going to pay attention to anything else. I told the bosses you wanted a Weatherby or something like that, something you could silence a little, but they wanted automatic fire. You understand that you won't really be able to see the guy, right? You understand that you'll have to spray the whole car in five or six seconds?"

He glanced at Terrier again. He seemed unhappy and exasperated, but he shrugged and settled into his seat, leaning his head against the back. Time passed. Every now and again, the travelers lighted a cigarette. Every now and then, Maubert babbled about the weather or other trivial subjects. Once they were on the highway, they stopped for coffee.

They made good time, reaching the Paris area in the wee hours of the morning. They parked the Estafette in an underground garage at Orly airport before going on to the PLM hotel. They went up without checking in. Maubert knocked on the door of a room. The short guy with black eyes opened the door, his eyelids puffy with sleep and his gray overcoat rumpled. He greeted Maubert and Terrier with a nod and left right away. Maubert hung the "Do Not Disturb" sign on the knob before closing the door.

Terrier woke up a little after eleven o'clock on the day of the planned assassination. In his underwear, he sat for a moment on the edge of his bed, slowly rubbing his belly. Through the half-open door of the bathroom came the light buzz of an electric razor. Then Maubert came out of the bathroom, in shirtsleeves. He wore an S&W .38 in a beige cloth shoulder holster. Terrier took his turn in the bathroom. He stayed a long time under the hot shower with his eyes closed and his lips shut tight. When he came back out into the room, the short guy with black eyes was sitting in an armchair. Maubert was waiting, standing against a wall. His weapon was now concealed by his jacket.

"Nothing else?" he asked.

"No," said the short guy.

"Don't you ever take your overcoat off?"

"Yes. Sometimes."

Maubert shrugged. He and Terrier went out and, after eating grilled pork in an airport restaurant, spent the afternoon in a movie theater, where they distractedly and successively watched an American crime story with Charles Bronson, a French crime story with Alain Delon, and a Walt Disney animated feature. Night had fallen when the two men came out of the cinema complex. They went to dinner. This time, while Maubert as usual ate heartily, Terrier hardly touched a thing. His companion, instead of babbling, was silent almost the whole time.

"I suppose you know you're not exactly what you might call a fun guy," said Maubert after dinner as he nursed a big tulip-shaped glass of extra-fine cognac. "This not-talking thing doesn't help at all—you should see a doctor, you know. Anyway, I don't get the impression you'd have a lot to say. You're a real pain. I'd really like to know what goes through your head."

Terrier raised his eyebrows. He smiled slightly. Maubert sighed disgustedly.

"It's time to go," he said.

They got the Estafette out of the underground garage and drove toward Paris, which they reached around ten-thirty in the evening. When they passed through the Porte de Versailles, Terrier turned for a moment to contemplate the façades of Boulevard Lefebvre, where he had once lived. Then, via Rue de Vaugirard and Les Invalides, the Estafette reached the Seine and the Champs-Elysées roundabout, where they made a hairpin turn into Avenue Montaigne. The van entered the left-hand service road. Maubert peered through the windshield. He braked and flashed the headlights. Immediately, a Lincoln in a marked-out parking space illuminated its parking lights and its turn signal. It backed up, pulled out, and left. Maubert gave a grunt of satisfaction and parked the Estafette in the freed space.

"There we are," he said.

He turned off the lights, opened a compartment under the dashboard, and brought out four curved magazines.

"There's four of them," he observed. "I don't think you'll need all that, but. . . . " His voice trailed off. "One hundred and twenty rounds," he added cheerfully.

The two men slipped into the back of the little van. Terrier assembled the Valmet. He examined the magazines, then inserted one into the weapon, which he weighed up intently. His fingers mechanically palpated the mechanisms.

"It works like a Kalashnikov, doesn't it?" asked Maubert.

Terrier nodded vaguely, as if to say, yes, more or less, you could say that. He continued to handle the weapon. He shouldered it several times, bringing the barrel to bear in the same motion. He smiled at Maubert and nodded. Leaning over the seatbacks, Maubert turned the radio on low and tuned it to France Inter, which sometimes gave a little more information than other stations when it came to diplomatic news and gossip about statesmen. The short eleven o'clock bulletin was indeed just starting, but Sheik Hakim's visit to France was mentioned only briefly, without details. Maubert turned off the radio. He went back to Terrier, who was sitting on the cold metal floor and cradling the assault rifle. The man with the blond mustache opened a kind of hold in the side of the van and extracted a long, flat portable transceiver, a kind of walkie-talkie. He drew out some tens of centimeters of antenna in the darkness of the van and flipped a switch.

"Goldfish." he said. "In position. Lookout, go ahead." He twiddled something.

A wave of static was heard, in the midst of which a low crackle might have included the words: "Lookout. Understood, Goldfish. Hold on. Silence. Out."

Maubert put the set on the metal floor and sat down facing Terrier. The two men could barely see each other in the darkness of the van. The orange glare of the urban lighting illuminated the avenue well; it illuminated the interior of the cab acceptably; but it filtered only indirectly into the back of the Estafette. Terrier and Maubert were silent and motionless for a long while. About eleven-thirty, Maubert lighted a cigarette, holding his pack out to Terrier, who shook his head.

"Basically," said Maubert, "anyone could do your job. I bet they pay you well, but anyone could do it. You're paid for running the risk. For the responsibility. I mean, if you're nabbed one day, you're nabbed as a killer—that's what I mean when I say 'risk.' They don't pay you for your skills."

With both hands, Terrier offered Maubert the Valmet in the dark. Maubert laughed nervously and shook his head. He drew on his cigarette as Terrier placed the assault rifle back on his lap and smiled.

"No, thanks," said Maubert. "Besides. . . . " He thought for a moment. "Besides, you're certainly paid for your reflexes, too. Think about it, I've never killed anyone. I mean, not in cold blood. In war, yes." He spoke softly in the darkness out of caution. For one thing, every time the lights turned green, traffic surged down the avenue; for another, the occasional pedestrian hastened through the freezing night right past the Estafette. "I'm sure I'd be capable of killing in cold blood. But if something went wrong, I don't know how I'd react. You always have the right reflexes, don't you? That's why they pay you so much, right?"

In the darkness, Terrier shrugged. Maubert was quiet for a moment. Then:

"What do I open so you can shoot?"

Terrier leaned forward and stretched out an arm. He tapped on one of the two lower panels of the back of the van as if he were knocking softly to be let in, then he leaned back again. Maubert nodded.

"Your girl really made a play for me, you know," he said abruptly. He cleared his throat. "I don't know anything about your relationship. But she offered herself openly, you know what I mean? As a general rule, it's not my style to fuck around on a job. But this was different. She took me by surprise. I mean, it was something violent. She's a little nuts, I have to say."

The walkie-talkie on the metal floor began spitting out incomprehensible words. Maubert picked it right up.

"Goldfish," he said. "Repeat."

He listened. He squinted. He put the set down.

"The target is early," he said worriedly. "He's on his way."

It was close to midnight. Traffic had increased after the movies had let out. Here and there, along the part of the avenue near the roundabout, small groups of pedestrians and couples were returning to their cars, starting their engines, and letting them warm up before setting off.

"Shit, what a fuck-up," said Maubert.

Terrier had crossed his arms and slipped his fingers under his armpits. Maubert quickly opened the rear door that Terrier had designated.

"You haven't attached the sight," he said anxiously.

Terrier shrugged again. He unfolded his arms and flexed his fingers. Then he stretched out on the metal floor and raised the Valmet. The position of the prone gunman was perfect. He had a clear view of the roundabout and the first two hundred meters of Avenue Montaigne. Maubert quickly moved back past Terrier's extended body and positioned himself behind the shooter. A full minute passed. Then the sound of whistles filled the crossroads. And, exactly as Maubert had described it earlier, four motorcycle cops bolted from the roundabout, followed by a Citroën SM, a Citroën Pallas, and another Citroën SM. Terrier aimed his weapon at the Citroën Pallas as soon as he saw it. The convoy turned into the avenue. All of a sudden, Terrier rolled over on his back. He glimpsed Maubert leaning over him with the Smith & Wesson in his hand. With all his strength, Terrier smashed the butt of his weapon into the man's testicles. Maubert's face was incredibly contorted; he doubled up. Swinging the butt down, Terrier knocked the revolver from his hand. Then he grabbed the crumpling, mustachioed man by the ears and beat his face against the floor. At that instant, at least three automatic weapons let loose along the avenue. Dropping the unconscious Maubert, Terrier jumped over the seatbacks and took the wheel of the Estafette. As he started up, he saw out of the corner of his eye that one of the motorcycle cops had fallen and that the other three were desperately trying to stop. An out-of-control Citroën SM, its windshield shattered, plowed into one of them and sent him sailing into the gutter before it climbed the sidewalk and hit a tree. Tires screeching, the Pallas zigzagged, and bullet holes appeared in its side as it successfully avoided the two unharmed motorcycle cops by veering from side to side almost on two wheels; eventually, it made its escape and snaked off toward Place de l'Alma. Meanwhile, the second SM spun around in the middle of the avenue and came to rest against the traffic island at the mouth of Rue Bayard. Two or three concealed shooters continued spraying, and the windows of the second SM crumbled. There were no tracer bullets.

During these same few seconds, the Estafette had started. Engine roaring, it tore out of its parking place, turned into the service road, and immediately swerved into Rue Bayard, which it took in the wrong direction. A Citroën 2CV was approaching slowly. Terrier turned on the headlights and accelerated. The little car swerved abruptly and jammed itself between two vehicles parked in front of Radio Luxembourg. The Estafette ripped off one of the little car's fenders as it went by and continued on toward the east, still accelerating. Far behind, at the junction of Avenue Montaigne and Rue Bayard, gunfire could still be heard, but it was more and more sporadic.

Terrier turned left at the end of Rue Bayard, which brought him back to the Champs-Elysées roundabout. He immediately turned right, then right again a little farther on; finally, he took the expressway along the Right Bank. From time to time he glanced at Maubert, who lay on the floor of the van. The man seemed to be unconscious. Terrier had taken Maubert's .38 and stuck it in his pocket. The Valmet assault rifle was propped next to him on the passenger seat.

Past Châtelet, the Estafette stopped for a red light. Terrier quickly took advantage of the moment to climb into the back, where Maubert was beginning to stir. He hit him hard in the back of the head with the butt of the Smith & Wesson before returning to the wheel and setting off again. Maubert had stopped moving. Terrier turned the radio back on. Between various pieces of light music, a woman with a pensive and lascivious voice chewed the fat with more or less forlorn human beings who called her on the phone to tell her that they loved Tchaikovsky or that they were sad or things of that sort. Terrier's face was covered in sweat, and his lips were in continual motion.

He left the expressway at the exit for the Gare de Lyon. He reached Place de la Nation, then came to Vincennes—not the park with its frequent police patrols, but the residential streets. He parked in a dark, narrow street. He went into the back of the van, sat Maubert up against the wall, and aimed the beam of the rubber-covered flashlight in his eyes. He pinched his cheeks and slapped him several times. Maubert half opened his eyes. He seemed drowsy. He couldn't focus. Terrier, who still had Anne's notebook and its little pencil, scribbled something and thrust it under Maubert's nose. The mustachioed man appeared to try and concentrate. His eyes were unfocused, and he kept blinking. He couldn't manage to read. Terrier lost his patience. He stuck the short barrel of the Smith & Wesson in Maubert's mouth, knocking him in the teeth.

"Unh! Unh!" said Maubert, his head pressed against the steel side of the Estafette.

Terrier ripped the .38 from the soft mouth, scraping a lip as he did so with the front sight. He kicked Maubert in the belly to encourage him.

"I feel sick," said Maubert.

Terrier kicked him again. Maubert grimaced.

"I might have a concussion," he said in a thick voice.

"What do you want? No, wait. Just my luck to be interrogated by someone who doesn't ask any questions. . . . " Terrier struck his knee with the barrel of the revolver. Wincing, Maubert tucked his leg under him. "You were supposed to shoot," he said reproachfully. "You were supposed to shoot the camel jockey. Then and only then was I supposed to shoot you in the head. I was supposed to say. . . . " He broke off. He seemed to be struggling to speak. Suddenly, his eyes closed and he went limp. He slid quietly to the floor.

With a thumb, Terrier raised first one of Maubert's eyelids and then the other. Maubert showed no ocular reflexes. Terrier checked his pulse. The heart had stopped. Terrier stood up and spat on the corpse. He was trembling a little.

After he had taken the ring road and was driving down the Autoroute du Sud, he heard the one o'clock news, which reported an assassination attempt against the OPEC representative, who had escaped unscathed. Terrier was approaching the Nemours exit, and he began slowing down in order to leave the highway and head for Larchant. He had a rather satisfied expression on his face.

18

Impeccably dressed in a beige three-piece suit, a shirt with pale blue stripes and a tab collar with a pin, and a royal-blue silk tie, Stanley, the black man, stood motionless in the middle of the dining room of his pied-à-terre. His feet were in a cardboard box on whose side could be read the word "VITTEL." His hands were cuffed tightly behind his back. A wide piece of white adhesive tape covered his mouth. Sweat ran slowly and regularly down the very black skin of his face, and dark haloes had begun forming under his armpits.

In a corner of the room, a hi-fi system played jazz and American popular music rather loudly: the automatic changer played Charlie Parker, Frank Sinatra, the Dizzy Gillespie big band, Ray Charles, etc., in succession. At times, Stanley seemed to shiver. At one moment, violent trembling seized his left leg. He closed his eyes and breathed deeply; the trembling stopped; he opened his eyes again and sighed.

After passing through Larchant, Terrier turned into the narrow, badly paved road that led to Stanley's weekend house. A few hundred meters down, he pulled the two right-hand wheels up onto the shoulder. The low branches lashed against the body of the Estafette. Leaving the engine running, Terrier halted and switched off the parking lights. Not a cloud in the sky, and the night was perfectly clear. Terrier waited till his eyes had adjusted to the semidarkness. Then, feeling his way in the back of the van, he put the walkie-talkie on receive. He waited again as he took the sling from the narrow case, which also contained other accessories, and attached it to the assault rifle. All that came from the little radio was an indistinct background hum, occasionally punctuated by a burst of static.

About one-forty-five, Terrier took the wheel again. Without turning on the headlights, he very slowly covered a few hundred meters. He narrowed his eyes to make out the road before him. The rifle was to his right on the floor of the cab, the walkie-talkie on the passenger seat. The Estafette made very little noise because the man had quickly slipped it into third gear and was barely touching the accelerator—just enough so the engine wouldn't stall.

Six or seven hundred meters before Stanley's house, Terrier spotted a clearing on the right among the firs and birches. He turned sharply in among the trees, mowing down a few saplings, then killed the ignition. The Estafette stood on packed dirt with sandstone showing through in places.

"Hey! . . . Hey! . . ." came a voice from the transceiver. The voice had a twang but was otherwise very distinct. "I think I see something."

"Then shut the fuck up," another voice hissed after a brief volley of static.

Terrier remained motionless in the cab. His lips were sealed. He had taken the .38 from his belt. The Estafette's engine cooled off quickly because of the cold outside: tiny sounds of crackling metal could be heard. The radio was silent, apart from the background hum. Terrier went back into motion: he slipped the revolver back into his belt, and the grip of the weapon bruised his stomach when he bent over to pick the Valmet up off the floor. He was delicately opening the door when the transceiver started up again.

"Hey!" said the first voice. "I got it wrong. I thought something was happening on the road, but there's zero out there."

"You're sure?"

"Positive."

"Fine, now shut the fuck up."

"What's the point of having walkie-talkies," the walkie-talkie said grumpily, "if we can't talk to each other?"

"You were told to just give a tap if you saw something. Shit! Are you going to shut up or not? Don't you understand that he might have a set, too, dickhead?

"Okay," the first voice said stiffly. "Okay."

After that, the set was silent.

Terrier waited a second, then he finished opening the door and got out of the Estafette. He was carrying the rifle on its sling, with the barrel down, so he moved rather swiftly through the woods. He swung his arms to the left and right at shoulder level to part the branches, which were almost invisible in the darkness. He held the .38 in his right hand and the Lyman scope in his left. He circled around to the back of Stanley's weekend house.

The house was a small concrete cube, with a basement garage on one side and a mansard roof. Behind the shutters, all the windows were lighted up. From where he was, at the edge of the bare ground encircling the house, Terrier could vaguely hear music.

He crouched at the edge of the woods. The low-hanging branches touched the wire fencing stretched between whitewashed cement posts. He had put the .38 down on a sandstone outcropping and was holding the Lyman scope in both hands. He very slowly scrutinized Stanley's house and its immediate vicinity. Then, standing back in order to be bothered less by the low-hanging branches, he pointed the apparatus in the direction of the road, along the line of the fence that he was next to. He couldn't make out much. Suddenly, there was a brief, weak red glow at the edge of the forest, near the road.

Terrier immediately put down the scope and took the Valmet off his shoulder. He unfastened the sling and slipped the revolver into his pants. Leaving rifle and scope behind, he began crawling along the fence. He crawled rapidly. The little noise that he made was inaudible because of the cold wind in the trees. After a few moments, Terrier found himself some ten meters from the empty road, and he made out the silhouette of a kneeling man in a light-colored parka, sheltered under a fir tree with his back to Terrier. The lookout was watching the road from his hiding place. A walkie-talkie and an M16 lay next to him on the sand. The man drew on his cigarette as he shielded it with his hand. Terrier got to his feet behind the man and rolled the ends of the Valmet's sling around his fists. He took three steps forward and, without a sound, throttled the smoker.

He left the corpse where it lay, after glancing at the face. It was the man who had followed him with *Le Monde diplomatique* in his pocket and later put the Bodyguard Airweight to his head in the hotel, in front of Anne, while she was naked. Passing through the interior of the forest, Terrier returned to the fence where he had left the Valmet and the scope. He stuffed the sights in the inside pocket of his jacket, slung his rifle on his shoulder, and, bent double, ran to the back of the enclosure, then scrambled up and over the fence and sprinted across the thirty meters of open ground that separated him from the house.

The rest of the house had almost no openings, the sole exceptions being the kitchen window and the bathroom skylight in the mansard roof. Terrier caught his breath and climbed the downspout at the corner of the house. From there, he hoisted himself up to the sill of the skylight. It had opaque glass and a wooden frame, and it was locked shut. Squatting on the sill, Terrier listened to the music coming up from the ground floor. It was Stanley's records that were being played. At present, it was the Dizzy Gillespie big band as recorded live at the Newport Jazz festival in the fifties. During a series of particularly aggressive riffs by the trumpet section, Terrier gave the skylight frame a good, hard kick. If he had not held onto the rain gutter with both hands, he would have lost his balance and fallen. He waited for another loud passage of music to give another kick. The screw of the latch was forced halfway out. Terrier pushed gently: the screw and the latch came apart and fell noiselessly on the thick bathroom rug below, and the skylight opened.

On the ground floor, in the middle of the dining room, Stanley was still standing in the Vittel box; he wore an agonized expression, and he was covered in sweat. His left thigh was trembling uncontrollably; he closed his eyes and grimaced; his jaws were working and his teeth grinding under the gag.

Taking care not to knock the Valmet against the frame of the skylight, Terrier inched his way through feet first and dropped down into the little room, between the bathtub and the sink. No lights were on in the bathroom, but the door was open onto the lighted hallway. Terrier picked up his assault rifle and stole a glance down the hallway. He pulled back immediately, took off his shoes, then advanced in his stocking feet.

The doors of the three bedrooms were shut. Near the bathroom, the hallway ended at a wall with one window set in it. The shutters were closed. In the other direction, the hallway continued as a balcony overlooking the dining room. Just as before in the Rue Varenne duplex, the short guy with the black eyes and the rumpled overcoat stood looking down from the balcony, with his elbows on the railing. A walkie-talkie sat next to him on the natural pine floor, and in his right hand was a Star BKM automatic pistol whose barrel rested in the crook of his left arm.

Terrier advanced very slowly down the hallway. His sweat-dampened socks did not slip on the wooden floor. He aimed the Valmet at the short guy. Out of the corner of his eye, the short guy noticed the slight movement in the hallway at the edge of his field of vision, and he immediately pressed the trigger of his automatic, which was already pointing in that direction. The 9mm bullet sent up a spray of pine splinters two meters from Terrier, who thereupon let loose with four-teen rounds at the short guy, who was busy throwing himself on his belly. Since Terrier was aiming at his legs, the short guy was almost cut in two lengthwise by the 7.62mm bullets.

The reports, especially those of the powerful automatic rifle, had reverberated deafeningly in the hallway, and the air reeked of cordite. Terrier quickly pulled back into the door-way of the bathroom and waited. Downstairs, the Dizzy Gillespie record was over, and the automatic changer clicked. The short guy's corpse was bleeding all over. He had pieces of his brains in his ear and between his teeth. The walkie-talkie, though intact, was silent. Not a sound came from the bed-room. No door opened. Terrier sighed and poked at his ear with his little finger. Downstairs, the record player clicked again, and Ray Charles began enthusiastically to shout halle-lujah, he loved her so.

After a moment, Terrier put his shoes back on and went and opened the doors of the bedrooms, taking precautions.

The rooms were all lit up, but no one was inside. In the first room, the bed was unmade, men's clothing was thrown over a seatback, and on a little desk was a framed photograph of two black men in their sixties, dressed up in their Sunday best. The second room had not been occupied recently. The mattress on the bed was bare. A vacuum cleaner and boxes of old magazines were set against one wall. There was dust on the furniture. In the third, Terrier found blond hair on the rumpled bed and an empty cognac bottle lying in the corner. Another bottle had been thrown at the door; the pieces were on the floor, and cognac had splattered the wall and run down to the floor.

Holding the Valmet out in front of him, Terrier advanced along the balcony. With one shoulder against the corner of a wall, he surveyed the dining room below, where Stanley, standing in the noncarbonated mineral-water box, his stocking feet on a squat metallic cylinder reminiscent of a pressure cooker, strained his neck muscles to see behind him. He saw Terrier on the balcony at the head of the flight of stairs leading down to the dining room. Stanley groaned sharply behind his gag. The muscles tightened in Terrier's neck. He groaned like Stanley. Then he came quickly down the stairs, keeping the Valmet at the ready and glancing warily this way and that.

Without for the moment concerning himself with Stanley, who was shaking, sweating, and groaning, Terrier went briskly through the ground-floor rooms and found no one. He came back to Stanley and ripped off his adhesive-tape gag.

"I'm standing on a mine," said Stanley.

Terrier gave him a perplexed look. Then he raised his eyebrows and proceeded to examine the flat cylinder of dull metal on which Stanley stood trembling in his stocking feet.

"My left heel is on the detonator," said Stanley. "It was armed by my stepping on it. They made me step on it." A terrible trembling ran up and down his left leg. "If I raise my foot, it goes off. I can't hold on much longer. Hurry up—go to the kitchen and get a knife from the table drawer."

Terrier rushed to the kitchen, opened the table drawer, found a carving knife, and returned to Stanley.

"I'll do it myself," said the black man. "It's too dangerous. We'll have to cut the chain of the handcuffs. Go down in the cellar. There's a toolbox. Bring up the wire cutters."

Terrier put a knee on the floor near the Vittel box, set down the Valmet, and crouched down to examine the box and Stanley's feet.

"No, stop, no, shit," said Stanley. "Go get the wire cutters. Please, Christian—it's too dangerous."

Holding the knife handle in one hand and the point of the blade in the other, Terrier slid the knife under the black man's left foot, slowly interposing the blade between the man's heel and the detonator. The heel was trembling. Sweat ran down Stanley's face. Once the blade was interposed between the detonator and the foot, Terrier raised his eyes toward Stanley and nodded and smiled. Stanley dropped to the floor. He curled up, then stretched out, then curled up again. His muscles quivered all over, and suddenly he urinated in his impeccable trousers. With one knee on the floor, Terrier looked at him and kept the blade of the knife pressed against the detonator.

"I've just taken a piss," observed Stanley. "What fucking bastards. I think they've got your chick, you know. They got the jump on me late in the afternoon. I think they took her away about an hour ago. They put me here, on this thing." He shook his head. "What fucking bastards," he repeated. All at once, he seemed to grasp Terrier's position; he moved quickly then, bending his knees, passing his handcuffed wrists under his heels, and then standing back up, with his hands in front of him. "Wait," he exclaimed uselessly. "We have to put something on the blade, something heavy. I have some bricks in the cellar. Will you go down? Bring me up the wire cutters, too. My legs have turned to jelly. Go on—I'll hold the knife."

On all fours near the Vittel box, Stanley pressed both fists down onto the blade. His fists were trembling. He half smiled at Terrier, who had extricated himself and was heading toward the cellar.

"You're no chatterbox," he observed. "Hurry up—I've got the shakes, my friend."

As Terrier was starting down the cellar stairs, Stanley swore with surprise, and then the mine exploded. It was a powerful mine. The weekend house was fragile. The whole interior was blown up and all the windows shattered. The bearing walls and the roof then began to collapse piece by piece, just as matter collapses, or so they say, in the hearts of distant stars.

The shock had flung Terrier to the bottom of the cellar stairs—he landed flat on his hands and knees on the irregular ground strewn with coal dust. Grains of coal were embedded in his palms. An avalanche of debris came tumbling after him down the stairs. Kilos of broken boards and pieces of brick struck Terrier's back and head. Terrier got right back up. With debris falling all around him, he energetically climbed up the steps, slipping in the rubble and the fragments of laths, in the midst of a thick cloud of smoke and diverse particulate matter. His lips moved and uttered a sort of low squeak. He rapidly traversed what remained of the dining room. Around him, sections of the roof and walls solemnly collapsed and struck the ground with dull thuds and rebounded. Terrier stepped over the twisted, useless Valmet, almost trod on Stanley's red-and-white thoracic cage, and left the house by way of the back wall. He must have run back to the Estafette in a matter of seconds. He started the vehicle, backed up, and then set off again toward the highway.

19

Shortly after three in the morning, Martin Terrier entered Paris via the Porte d'Italie at the wheel of a stolen car, a white Peugeot 504. He had gotten rid of Maubert's body by leaving it under a truck parked on a street in Fresnes. Before doing so, he had gone through Maubert's pockets because he needed a little money. As for the various cards decorated with the French flag—they bore Maubert's photo and the name François Guénaud, along with the information that he belonged to the DST and other, less official services—Terrier had left them, after a moment's hesitation, in the dead man's wallet.

He had left the Estafette in Bagneux, where he had stolen the 504. He kept Maubert's .38 and the transceiver that communicated nothing. The 504 was equipped with a radio and cassette player, but the three o'clock news said nothing more than the one o'clock news, stating only that the assassination attempt against Sheik Hakim would make the headlines of all the morning papers—except for the sports paper, *L'Equipe.*

Traffic was light in Paris at that hour. Terrier headed toward Montparnasse. He noticed no unusual police activity.

A bar was open in Rue du Départ. Terrier entered around three-thirty. He went to the counter and handed the bartender a scrap of paper. The bartender frowned, then read what was written in pencil on the scrap of paper. He nodded and gave Terrier a grimace of sympathy. While the man bustled about, Terrier glanced around the room, but there was nothing to see except two men in a drunken stupor, a haggard semi-professional whore, and, on the tile floor, a layer of sawdust and cigarette butts.

In Rue La Boétie, in the offices of Impex Films International, men in dark clothing waited in the darkness with their revolvers.

In Rue du Départ, the bartender set before Terrier a small draft beer and a snifter containing vodka, two ice cubes, and a few drops of lemon juice.

"Careful with the mix," he said. "It can do you in." And since Terrier didn't react, the bartender added: "You're not deaf, too, are you? Don't tell me you're a deaf-mute!"

Terrier shook his head.

"Just mute, huh?" said the other man, wagging his head in a wise but pathetic way. "Maybe you just don't feel like having people talk to you?"

Terrier shrugged. He picked up the beer glass, knocked it lightly against the glass of vodka next to it, and took a swallow of beer. It was rather good but too cold.

"There are nights," said the bartender, "when I would love to be deaf myself." He sighed. "Well, that's how it is." And he went to sit down on a stool behind the cash register.

In Rue de Varenne, the doorbell resounded in the vast gray-and-white duplex full of ultramodern furniture and Pop, Op, and kinetic art. In the courtyard, the name "Lionel Perdrix" appeared on a framed visiting card above the doorbell.

"I don't believe it!" exclaimed Lionel Perdrix's bedmate in a tone of disgust.

On the night table, the digital clock read "3:46." Perdrix interrupted his movements. Someone rang the doorbell again. Perdrix disengaged, got out of bed, and left the bedroom, pulling on a white terry-cloth bathrobe. He was a short, pudgy man in his forties, with incipient baldness and bloodshot eyes. He was out of breath. While he was hurrying to the door, the bell rang again.

"Okay! Okay! What is it?"

Through the peephole in the white-lacquered door, he saw Cox and other silhouettes in coats or raincoats. His face took on a worried look. He hastened to unlock the door. Cox and three other men came right in, almost knocking into him. One man closed the door. The two others climbed the short flight of stairs to the duplex.

"Is there someone with you?" asked Cox.

"Yes, but. . . . "

"A girl?"

"Yes. Hey, what's going on? You told me it was all over. You told me that you would never use my apartment again. And, anyway, why didn't you call first?"

Cox didn't answer. He was looking toward the upstairs, whence a feminine voice cried out in protest. Perdrix started to go up, but the man who had closed the door held him by the arm.

"Look, I demand to know what's going on!"

Cox didn't answer. He pulled a Nuts bar from his pocket, tore away half the wrapping, and bit into the candy. The two scouts reappeared.

"There's a young woman in the bedroom, that's all," one of them reported.

Cox went up the stairs, and Perdrix followed, grumbling that it was all crazy, with the last guy still holding him by the arm; in the other hand the guy carried a case. Once they were upstairs, he released Perdrix's arm, put the case on the painted floor, and opened it: it contained three Ingram M11 machine pistols with silencers and night-vision sights. Perdrix's teeth began chattering. He was looking at the weapons. He automatically brought one hand to his jaw to arrest the trembling.

"But what are you doing?" he asked in a shrill voice.

"The bathroom is the only room without windows," said one of the scouts.

"Take the mattress from the bedroom and put it in the bathroom," Cox ordered. He turned to Perdrix. "Stop trembling. These weapons aren't for killing you. They're for your protection. You and your girlfriend have to stay in the bathroom the rest of the night. My men will stay here to protect you."

"I don't need protection. I'm not in danger," protested Perdrix through chattering teeth.

"Yes, you are," said Cox. "You know that I use your apartment for meetings. . . . "

"I don't know anything. I don't want to know anything. Go away, I beg you." Perdrix put his head in his hands. He may have been trying to block his ears with his palms.

"Someone dangerous is trying to find me," Cox explained reassuringly. "He doesn't know how to find me. But he knows where you live. Now you're going to shut yourself in the bathroom with your girlfriend, and my men will protect you."

"Who are these madmen?" shouted Perdrix's bedmate who had rushed out onto the balcony, wrapped in a sheet. (Meanwhile, the two scouts were dutifully carrying the mattress into the bathroom.)

"I'm calling the police," Perdrix told Cox.

"No," said Cox. "You're going to give me a radio so I can listen to the four o'clock news. And then you'll go upstairs and shut yourself in."

"Fine," said Perdrix. He went reluctantly toward the staircase that led to the balcony. He waved in the general direction of a hi-fi system and its tuner on the shelves of one wall.

"There's the radio," he said weakly.

He went up and shut himself in the bathroom with his girlfriend. Through the door, one could vaguely hear the girl protesting vociferously and the man responding in a spineless way. Cox's three men took their Ingram M11s and posted themselves at the windows. Cox turned on the radio.

"I'll listen to the news, then I'll go," he announced. "If he shows up here, don't miss."

He waited for four o'clock, finishing his Nuts bar.

In Rue du Départ, Martin clinked glasses once more with the untouched glass of vodka, then he downed his beer, collected his change, and left. After a minute or two, the bartender picked up the glass of vodka, shrugged, and drank it. Then he summarily washed the beer glass and the snifter. Meanwhile, Terrier had reached the 504. He turned on the radio and listened to the four o'clock news. The police had now identified the author of the failed assassination attempt against Sheik Hakim: he was a person known in international terrorist circles, one Martin Terrier, alias "Monsieur Christian." This killer, of French nationality, but in possession of several foreign passports, had been trained by the KGB in its special school in Odessa, then in the Palestinian camps and by the Cuban DGI. He had left his tracks in Africa, Italy, and South America. Many assassinations could be attributed to him, notably the killing of Luigi Rossi, an arms dealer identified as a "traitor" by the Red Brigades and, most recently, the execution in England of Marshall Dubofsky, likewise denounced by the Provisional IRA. Interviewed by telephone, Principal Commissioner Poilphard had declared: "He's big game, very big game."

Seated in the darkness of the 504, Martin Terrier listened

attentively to this news. His haggard face at first registered great perplexity; then it registered worry, thoughtfulness, or whatever other movements of consciousness that might cause his face to look as it did. Once the news was over, the man started his engine.

20

Rue de Varenne is quiet at four o'clock in the morning, especially in cold weather, and right then the temperature was no more than one or two degrees above freezing. The porte cocheres of the large town houses were shut. The security guards and doormen to be seen there during the day, in the entrances to ministerial buildings and government offices, had disappeared. The odd car or two sped by at rare intervals.

Cox left furtively and quickly at five after four in a black Citroën SM driven by a Eurasian man.

Martin Terrier appeared a quarter of an hour later, hands in pockets, coming around the corner from a side street about two hundred meters from Lionel Perdrix's place. He walked quickly, a little hunched over and with his collar turned up. All kinds of private cars were parked along the sidewalk: they were empty. Near Lionel Perdrix's home was a Volkswagen minibus; curtains hung in its back windows. Terrier came to the entrance of a building about a hundred meters farther down, on the other side of the street. He buzzed the door open, went inside, switched on the timer lights, went into the hall, turned, went through a self-closing door, and started up a staircase with wine-colored carpeting. He climbed up to the top floor and went down a corridor with a sloping ceiling and a row of flimsy doors along one side. His face was haggard. When he arrived at the last door, he took out his Swiss Army knife and silently jimmied the cheap lock. He went in, turned on the lights, and punched the jaw of the young girl in pajamas who had sat bolt upright in her bed and was opening her eyes to see and her mouth to scream. She instantly fell back on her pillow—

blonde, short, plump, and knocked unconscious. Terrier closed the door.

The man crossed the small room in two steps and looked out a mansard window with cretonne curtains. He had a view of Rue de Varenne and, notably, of Perdrix's building. With a contented expression, he went back toward the unconscious girl and rummaged through the three drawers of a white wooden chest. He used two pairs of woolen pajama bottoms to tie up the little blonde and a stocking and a third pair of pajama bottoms to gag and blindfold her.

He straightened up and looked around the place. The furniture was very basic: a table, a chair, a hot plate, a sink. On the floor were a record player and a few pop music records. On the wall was a movie poster of Jane Fonda in *Barbarella.* Postcards from distant lands were tacked up around a circular mirror. The clothes in the chest of drawers and the small wardrobe were cheap. Near the bed, the alarm clock was set for seven-fifteen. Terrier picked up the unconscious girl and deposited her on the floor. He took off his shoes and his sheepskin jacket, turned off the lights, and slipped into the warm bed. He quickly fell asleep.

When the alarm went off, the man immediately got up. The girl on the floor wriggled and groaned. She went quiet and rigid when she heard him moving around in the room. Terrier went straight to the mansard window. Aside from the numerous vehicles using Rue de Varenne, nothing was happening in front of Perdrix's building. The minibus was still in the same place. Terrier heated water in a pot. He went and got the Lyman scope from the inside pocket of his jacket and, while the water was heating, watched more carefully.

On the floor, the dumpy blonde began wriggling and

groaning again. Terrier looked at her with annoyance. He rummaged through the table drawer and found a nylon-tipped marker and a piece of paper. A short while later, the girl felt someone pulling her up by the hair. The blindfold was removed, and the knee of her aggressor rested against her back. She saw a hand holding up a piece of paper with a hastily written inscription in capital letters: "NO HARM WILL COME TO YOU. BE QUIET. YOU WILL NOT BE ROBBED OR RAPED OR KILLED OR ANYTHING. PLEASE BE NICE AND PATIENT." Then the blindfold was put back and tightened, and Terrier laid the blonde down and hurried off to the hot plate, because the water was about to boil. He made himself three cups of instant coffee and drank them with jam and bread. He ate and drank standing up, listening to the little radio turned down low and watching Lionel Perdrix's building. News bulletins were frequent at this time of day. That morning there was much talk of the assassination attempt on Sheik Hakim and of an airplane crash and the accidental death of a popular singer. About Martin Terrier, aka Monsieur Christian, there was the same biographical information that had been broadcast at four o'clock in the morning.

"Close collaboration between French and American intelligence services has led to the quick identification of the terrorist," said the newscaster. He then went on to say that the Soviet Union was seeking to stir up tension in the Persian Gulf, even though one might wonder whether such a policy was in the best interests of the Russians.

Terrier listened and watched.

About eight o'clock, Cox's surveillance team was relieved: six men arrived in two sedans; four of the men went into Lionel Perdrix's building; the other two got into the minibus.

Four men left the building and two left the minibus; the night team drove off in the two sedans.

A little after nine o'clock, the dumpy blonde began squirming and groaning again on the floor. Terrier gave her a carefully judged kick in the side, after which she kept still. Half an hour later, Terrier heard her crying indistinctly through the gag, and he noticed that she had urinated. She stopped crying a few minutes later. As if the prisoner had given him an idea, the killer pissed in the sink, then he smoked a Winston from a packet he had found on the table. He continued to watch. Silence had returned to the hallway; between seven-thirty and nine there had been noise, slamming doors, hurrying footsteps.

A black SM arrived in Rue de Varenne and pulled up in front of the porte cochere of Lionel Perdrix's building. The driver got out, leaving the engine running: the exhaust pipe released vapor into the cold air. The man was the Eurasian who had driven Cox the night before and Terrier and Anne another day. Terrier's muscles tensed. The Eurasian knocked on the rear door of the minibus. It half opened. There was talk. Terrier slipped on his jacket. He left the room and hurried to the staircase. On the floor of the cold little room, blondie was again vainly twisting and turning about; she was reflected in the round mirror, between the postcards from distant lands. Lionel Perdrix and his girlfriend appeared on the sidewalk along Rue de Varenne. Both seemed to be in a foul mood; they were flanked by two of Cox's men. The Eurasian signaled to them. The couple got into the SM. The Eurasian took the wheel.

"Where to?"

"To the Maison de la Radio."

"Hey!" said the girl.

"We'll drop the young lady at the first taxi stand," Perdrix said to the Eurasian as he was pulling out. The male passenger turned to the female passenger. "Listen, I'm sorry," he said. "I'm late, thanks to their foolishness." He looked anxiously at his watch. "Don't you realize that we're on the air in twenty minutes? Do you have money for a taxi?"

"Yes," the girl said furiously. "That's fine."

The occupants of the SM remained silent till reaching the Esplanade des Invalides, where the automobile halted and the girl got out. The Eurasian headed west, along the Seine.

"How long is this charade going to continue?" Perdrix asked him.

"What charade?"

"Putting guards in my house and spending an hour arguing about whether to let me go to work and having me driven around and . . . and. . . . " Perdrix took a deep breath as he tried to find his words. "How long is this going to continue?" he repeated.

"I don't know anything about anything," said the Eurasian. "I do what I'm told. I have no idea."

"I'm going to be late," said Perdrix, sounding shocked. "I work for Radio France Internationale, if you'd care to know, but that probably means nothing to you." He sniffed with disdain.

"Oh, yes," said the Eurasian man with a smile. "Broadcasts for niggers and chinks."

"Shit, you're the one to talk!"

The Eurasian frowned slightly.

"If you want to be on time, I advise you not to insult me."

Lionel Perdrix's eyes bulged and his mouth moved, but he

refrained from speaking and hunched himself up, looking furious. His breathing was noisy, and he sighed ostentatiously. The SM crossed the Seine, reached the Maison de la Radio, and parked.

"I'll wait here to take you back," said the driver. "How long will you be at it?"

"That's right, wait for me," sniggered Perdrix, jumping from the SM and running toward the curved, labyrinthine building with his briefcase clutched beneath his arm.

The Eurasian sniggered, too, and lighted a Camel. He picked up the telephone handset that was next to him on the seat, but he didn't put it to his ear right away. A Peugeot 504 was parking some distance away. A silhouette in a sheepskin jacket got out and walked away, with his collar turned up and his hands in his pockets.

"Sammy Chen here," said the Eurasian. "Everything's fine. Terrier's followed me, probably from Rue de Varenne. He's just parked. He's walking away on foot. I don't see him anymore." He smiled as he spoke softly, without taking the Camel from his delicate mouth. "He's sure to go around the Maison de la Radio and come up behind me. Make sure nothing nasty happens to me. But don't rush it, either, okay?" He chuckled. "I'm hanging up now," he said.

He hung up and waited. The rear door was still ajar; Lionel Perdrix hadn't bothered to slam it. Terrier slipped quickly into the SM and immediately put the barrel of the .38 against Sammy Chen's cerebellum. The Eurasian put both hands high on the steering wheel.

"I'm not making a move."

Terrier thrust a piece of paper in front of Sammy Chen's face. The Eurasian read it and seemed to be thinking.

"I don't know anything," he said. "I'm just a gofer. They don't tell me about that kind of stuff."

Terrier pocketed the note. Then with his left hand he seized the auricle of the chauffeur's left ear between his thumb and two fingers and tore it off. Sammy Chen howled. Terrier brought the barrel of his revolver down on Sammy Chen's skull, and the man collapsed onto the steering wheel. Blood spurted from the left side of his head. Pedestrians walked close by without paying attention to what was happening in the SM. Terrier threw the ripped-off ear on the floorboard and impatiently yanked his victim's hair. Sammy Chen moaned and thrashed about. Both back doors of the car opened at the same time. From one side a bearded man with blue eyes used both hands to point a Colt .45 automatic at Terrier's head. From the other side a black man in sunglasses hit him very hard on the biceps with a short iron bar. Terrier grunted, his arm folded, and his revolver fired in the air, making a hole the size of a large strawberry in the roof of the SM. The black man tore the .38 from Terrier and struck him on the knee with the iron bar. Terrier doubled over, grabbing his knee with both hands. The black man sat down to his left, the bearded man to his right. The bearded man jammed his big automatic in Terrier's ribs.

"Okay, let's get the hell out of here!" commanded the black man because a few passersby had stopped on hearing the gunshot and were now looking around for the source of the noise.

"Talk about luck," said Sammy Chen, sounding irritated. He started the car. "Look on the floor and see if my ear's there—this asshole ripped it off—there may be a way of sewing it back on."

As the SM was starting off, the black man searched around

on the floorboard and came up with the bloody relic. His eyebrows appeared above the frames of his glasses.

"I must be dreaming!" he exclaimed as he examined the red auricle. "Shit!" he added respectfully.

"This guy is really violent," said Sammy Chen with conviction.

The black man gave him his ear, and the mixed-race man wrapped it in a Kleenex and put it in his pocket as he drove. The SM was making for Neuilly. Terrier was hunched up, grimacing with pain. The black man and the bearded man searched him. They took away his Swiss Army knife and his Opinel knife—they even took his ballpoint pen. The bearded man read the piece of paper that Terrier had shown the Eurasian.

"Well, sure," he said with a disagreeable smile. "You'll see your bitch again. We're taking you to her now."

In Neuilly, the car pulled into the underground garage of a small building. They got out. The bearded man kept the barrel of his Colt jammed into Terrier's thorax. Terrier was limping. Sammy Chen tossed the black man the keys to the SM.

"Take the car. And tell them to fix the hole in the roof right away," he commanded. The black man seemed about to say something unpleasant. "I can't take it there like this," Chen explained amiably, indicating his torn-off ear and his cheek caked with drying blood.

The black man took the wheel of the SM and left the parking garage as Terrier and the other two men got into an elevator. On the top floor, the doors opened directly into a bright apartment. The furniture was Scandinavian, and the pictures were abstract.

"Go tell Cox," said Sammy Chen.

The bearded man gave him a doubtful glance, then went through a communicating door. Sammy Chen, his hands empty, remained alone with Terrier. Terrier eyed him.

"If you even try to sneak in a punch," said the mixed-race man, "I'll give you a *fumitsuki,* a *mae-tobi-geri,* a *hittsui-geri* in the balls, and then I'll really bust your chops and tear off both your ears. And plus . . ." (he suddenly began speaking very softly, between his teeth) ". . . and plus the situation is not what you think. I beg you to be patient." Terrier looked at him and knit his brow. "Sit down, you stupid jerk," Sammy Chen concluded in a loud voice.

Terrier sat down in an armchair. He clenched his fists when Anne came into the room. She was wearing a suit and a blouse that were not quite the right size; her face was drawn, and she had circles under her eyes. But otherwise she seemed in good shape. The bearded man held her by the right elbow, still holding the Colt automatic in his other hand. Then Cox, dressed in cotton trousers and a turtleneck sweater, came in, along with a stranger. The stranger was fortyish and well preserved; he was wearing a powder-blue three-piece suit. He had a strong face with a square jaw under rather short and wavy brown hair. He looked like a young senior executive.

"Well, so this is your Monsieur Christian," he said, contemplating Terrier. "How's it going?" he asked unexpectedly.

Terrier shrugged.

"He's mute," Cox observed glumly.

"Oh, yes, I'd forgotten."

"He's unusable."

"Let's sit, let's sit." The tone of voice of the man in the suit was benign but authoritative. Everyone sat down except for Sammy Chen, who moved away slightly and leaned against a wall. "You really can't speak?" Terrier shook his head. His gaze fixed on each of his interlocutors in turn, but kept returning to Cox.

"If he's mute, he's unusable," Cox repeated. "In any case, I don't like your idea at all."

"Do you understand what's happened to you these past weeks?" asked the man in the suit. "Or even in recent years, as one might say, in a sense?" Terrier nodded calmly. "That would surprise me," said Blue Suit. "It hardly matters, anyway. You are aware of the accusations against you. You know that, according to a consistent body of evidence, you are in the pay of the Russians—as much out of conviction as well as for love of money. The list of your victims indicates clearly enough on whose account you employed your talents as an assassin. Would you be willing to confirm this? Would you be willing to admit it in a court of law?"

Terrier's brow was furrowed. Cox gave an exasperated sigh, leaned over the low table of light-colored wood, and removed the cover of a round, stainless-steel container as big as a salad bowl. The container was full of salted almonds, peanuts, cashews, and raisins; Cox took a small handful and conveyed it to his mouth, breathing heavily, angrily.

"Well?" insisted Blue Suit.

"You can't have a mute testify," said Cox with his mouth full. Food particles sailed past his teeth. "Everyone will say that he's drugged or that he's been brainwashed. We have to do as I said at the start."

"Monsieur Cox's words don't carry any weight," the man in the powder-blue suit said to Terrier. "He set up the whole operation without authorization. He personally selected all your targets. The company approved all the contracts, but Cox never informed anyone that he was reserving you exclusively and systematically for the elimination of double agents. Cox played a kriegspiel to his own advantage." The man leaned forward. He looked Terrier in the eye. His gaze and his facial expression bespoke candor and trust. "Monsieur Cox created you. He created an assassin whose list of targets comprised only dubious characters who had shown us a few kindnesses or, at least, displayed a few weaknesses. Cox set up the operation against Sheikh Hakim entirely by himself. Do you understand? If you had been killed yesterday evening, as he had planned, you would have made the perfect corpse. Everything that you did before can be laid at the Russians' door or at the door of elements manipulated by the Russians. So the attack on Sheik Hakim can be as well. Do you understand that?"

Terrier nodded.

"It's certainly a nuisance that you're mute," said Blue Suit. "You can never know whether a man who doesn't speak is intelligent or stupid." He shook his head musingly, as if he had discovered a profound truth and was now contemplating it.

"He's an idiot," said Cox.

Terrier grew excited and gestured eloquently.

"Oh," said Blue Suit. "You want to express yourself. You want to write."

From his jacket he produced a very thin notebook and a tiny golden mechanical pencil and passed them over to Terrier, who began to scribble busily.

"Listen,' said Cox, "why do people create problems for themselves? That's exactly what you're doing." He looked spitefully at the man in the powder-blue suit. "When you say that I set up the operation against Sheikh Hakim by myself, you know you're flying blind."

"Oh, yes, I know, you have connections," said Blue Suit with disdain. "Foreign connections—precisely what we don't want."

Terrier returned his notebook. Blue Suit read it, raising his eyebrows. He chuckled and looked at Cox, then at Terrier, then once more at Cox.

"He hates you," he said. "And, well, he's not an idiot. He's ready to confirm everything, including the fact that he never did anything except obey his station chief."

"But," said Cox, "that's me." He seemed surprised.

"Yes," said Blue Suit. "Martin Terrier's claim is that he was manipulated by his station chief, who worked for the Russians. He's ready to confirm everything."

"Very funny," said Cox without smiling. From under his sweater he produced a Colt Commander, and Sammy Chen took two steps forward and tore the weapon from his hand.

"Thank you, Sammy," said Blue Suit. He smiled at Cox. "You've lost your reflexes, I see."

Cox looked stupefied. He stuffed his mouth with almonds and other junk from the steel container. Peanut fragments stuck to his lower lip. He shook his head. He stared into space.

"You know very well that I never. . . . "

"Well, yes, of course," said Blue Suit. "But someone has to carry the can. Martin Terrier will carry the can. But there'll be a little can for you, too. It will irritate your foreign connections, of course. But we don't want anything to do with your foreign connections. The company has had enough of your faction."

"It would be simpler for everyone to do as I said," muttered Cox as he dug in the container for more peanuts and almonds.

"Yes," said Blue Suit, "but we have Terrier alive. We'll kill two birds with one stone."

"That's what you think," said Cox, sounding assertive. From under the almonds and raisins and peanuts and salted hazelnuts he pulled out a tiny Lenz Lilliput automatic pistol and extended his arm and put the barrel of the weapon against Martin Terrier's temple and shot him in the head. Terrier opened his mouth wide, half raised his arms in the air, and slid to the bottom of his seat.

"The situation has just changed," observed Cox.

"Not so much, not so much," Terrier declared in a thick and obstinate voice as he got back up, with blood flowing from the hole in his head. It was only then that Anne began to scream.

21

Anne's scream was brief. It stopped short when Cox fired again, producing a sound like a hard slap. The second 4.25mm projectile penetrated Martin Terrier's left lung and lodged there. Martin Terrier's outstretched right arm swept through the air, and the palm of his hand struck the little pistol and knocked it from Cox's fingers and sent it flying to the far end of the room. The weapon landed at the foot of the wall and fetched up against the baseboard. Cox gave a sharp groan. He stumbled as he tried to jump over the low table. The hazelnuts and the rest were overturned. Cox fell to his hands and knees in the middle of the carpet. Continuing to groan with terror, he set off on all fours at an astonishing speed toward the tiny automatic. Terrier took four even quicker strides and picked up the weapon. He aimed it with both hands at Cox's sweat-covered forehead.

"What should I do? What should I do?" asked Sammy Chen with a distinct nervousness as he brandished the Colt Commander. He seemed uncertain whether or on whom he should open fire.

"Don't shoot! Don't shoot!" commanded Blue Suit in an even more nervous tone. When Cox had fired the second time at Terrier, Blue Suit had put his weight on his heels and forced the little sofa on which he sat to tip over backward; now he was down on his belly behind the overturned sofa. "No one do anything! Please!"

No one did anything. Everyone was almost motionless. Drops of perspiration ran into Cox's eyes. Resting on his elbows and knees, he raised his head as high as possible and seemed to be looking right down into the pistol barrel pointing between his eyes. There was a little blood in Terrier's hair, and a little more, of a brighter red, trickled from the corner of his mouth. The man seemed surprised and worried.

"Finish it," asked Cox. His voice was calm and subdued. "Come on," he said. "Come on. Come on. Finish it."

"I can't," said Martin Terrier.

He moved back slightly and leaned against the partition. The little automatic was still aimed between Cox's eyes.

"It's true. I can't do it," Terrier repeated.

From behind the overturned sofa, Blue Suit performed an urgent pantomime for Sammy Chen, who moved immediately to take the pistol from Terrier's hands—though it was not quick and not easy, for he had to twist the killer's fingers to make him release it, said fingers being clenched convulsively around the grip, the trigger, and the trigger guard of the weapon. At last, Sammy pocketed the Lilliput. Blue Suit got back to his feet.

"Go sit down, you damn fool," he said to Cox.

Cox went and sat down in a corner on the floor. A few moments later, he vomited in a fabulous way, as if he were disgorging everything he had swallowed for years. No one paid much attention to the phenomenon.

Meanwhile, Sammy Chen and Blue Suit had closely examined Terrier. Anne held back, pale faced.

"He's rigid," said Sammy Chen. "Maybe he should be given a calcium injection."

"Are you stupid or what?" Blue Suit asked angrily. "He has a bullet in the head and another in the lung. He's going to die."

"No way," said Terrier, who was still standing, leaning against the wall, with a hole in his head and a hole in his torso and blood from his lung foaming at the corners of his mouth. “No way!” he repeated, stamping his foot.

“In any case, he’s not mute anymore,” said Sammy Chen.

“I’m going to call. We may as well have him taken to the hospital—you never can tell, and it’s no skin off our nose,” said Blue Suit as he turned and made for the telephone.

“You’re beautiful,” said Terrier, looking at Anne. He seemed to have some difficulty in putting words together. “Beautiful,” he repeated. “Beautiful.”

“He’s not mute anymore, but he’s blabbering,” said Sammy Chen.

“Beautiful, beautiful.”

Terrier didn’t die. He was taken by ambulance to a hospital, where he spent nearly three hours on the operating table.

“The lung’s no problem,” the surgeon said afterward to the man in the blue suit. “The patient is in rather good physical condition, and, well, in short, I’m not going to bore you with technical details, but in this regard he’ll be like new. The real problem is the bullet in the brain.”

“You left it there?”

“If I tried to remove it, I’d kill him. It’s practically in the geometric center of the skull. I don’t know why it didn’t cause more obvious damage. This man should be dead or totally or partially paralyzed, or at least in a coma or something. In fact, his reflexes are normal, and his mind doesn’t seem to be affected. We observe only an episodic tendency to blabber. But only when he’s under sedation.”

“That’s strange, isn’t it?” asked Blue Suit.

“Very strange.”

“Can I see him?”

“Would tomorrow morning be all right?” asked the surgeon. “He’s resting at the moment. He’s sleeping, and he needs it.”

"Does he talk in his sleep?"

"As I said, every now and then he blabbers. Well, I call it blabbering. It's very strange."

"I want a tape recorder put in his room," said Blue Suit. "Voice activated. I'll bring you one. I want everything recorded. Even this blabbering or whatever you call it."

The next morning, the man in the blue suit found Martin Terrier in good shape, even though the professional killer was on a drip.

"I'm ready to cooperate with you," said Terrier. "I don't believe I'm going to die. And I don't think you're going to kill me. I can be useful to you, as I understand it. I'm willing. But under certain conditions."

"Okay, let's see about that," said Blue Suit.

They came to an agreement that same day. Thereafter, they had daily conversations, first at the hospital and then, beginning two weeks later, on an isolated estate, where Terrier was transferred during his convalescence. The property was spacious and luxurious, and not far from Montfort-l'Amaury. The house itself was surrounded by modest grounds enclosed by a wall. A few armed men provided the domestic service, and they patrolled the park with attack dogs. Anne was accommodated upstairs in the room next to Terrier's. This was one thing that the professional killer had demanded. He had also asked for Cox's head, but without great conviction; the request was refused. Cox was posted to South America, where he occupied a subordinate position in the company's Bogotá station for six months. Then he put both barrels of a shotgun in his mouth and pulled the two triggers with his big toe. Was he perhaps still looking for oral fulfillment when he placed the hollow cylinders of cold steel between his teeth? In any case, what he found was death, and he was buried once a specialist had reassembled the pieces of his head. His corpse was very skinny.

"Have you never thought of going back to work for the company?" Blue Suit asked Terrier during one of their interviews. A tape recorder was running in plain sight on the table. Blue Suit would sometimes stop it to speak in confidence with Terrier. Two hidden machines recorded everything that was said; other recorders were hidden in Terrier's and Anne's rooms.

"Isn't that what I'm doing now?"

"I mean, in your old job," said Blue Suit. He put the visible tape recorder on pause. "As a killer."

"That's impossible," said Terrier. "I've become incapable of killing. I realized it the day I caught those two bullets. I really wanted to kill Cox, but I couldn't do it. I think I could kill to defend myself or to defend Anne. Or if I was extremely angry. Otherwise, no."

"Martin Terrier is normal, inasmuch as the concept of normality is operative," explained one of the psychiatrists who were studiously examining the audiotapes.

"Everything confirms it," said the other psychologist. "Do you want to listen to a recording made Friday evening in the woman's room?"

"No, thanks. I know already. How do you interpret it?"

"Given that we don't have recourse to optical recordings, the interpretation is necessarily limited. Climax occurred three minutes after penetration, and that was preceded by one minute of foreplay."

"Isn't that extremely brief?" asked Blue Suit.

"Yes, of course, if we compare this behavior to that of cultivated and imaginative people like you and me. But it's very close to the American national average of the fifties."

"Excuse me," said the other psychiatrist, "but the study you're alluding to is open to challenge in terms of science, as you well know."

"Don't start arguing," commanded Blue Suit. "Have you analyzed the blabbering?"

"It's groaning," said the second psychiatrist. "The subject groans in his sleep."

"I'm more in favor of the term 'blabbering,'" said the first psychiatrist.

They started to bicker. To put an end to it, Blue Suit sent copies of all the sounds that Martin Terrier made in his sleep to company headquarters, not far from Washington, D.C. These recordings were subjected to lengthy examination by many people and many computers, with no tangible result.

After a few months, at the end of spring, Terrier stopped blabbering at night. He had slipped into a depression. He often spent hours drinking anisette and listening to Maria Callas records, after which he would fall into a stupor.

"You're going to publish a book of memoirs," Blue Suit told him one summer morning.

"You're not in your right mind," said Terrier. "I'm not capable of that. I can't write."

"It's already written," said Blue Suit as he sat down. He deposited a stack of photocopies on a round table. "I had one of our academics write it. I'll read it with you, and we'll correct the details. Improbabilities and inaccuracies must be avoided."

"You can hardly avoid inaccuracies!" Terrier laughed sadly.

"I'm speaking of verifiable inaccuracies. Those are the ones to avoid."

"Fine," said Terrier. "I'll do my best."

They spent more than twenty hours over the course of a week carefully examining the manuscript. Written in the first person, the work related just eight assassinations, which were ordered by Moscow, and gave many details on the training that Terrier was supposed to have received in Odessa and on the organization of the KGB and its ties with other secret services and with international terrorism. In the first chapter, the author recounted how in his adolescence he had espoused communist ideals. In the penultimate chapter, the narrator made a wrenching self-criticism. Abjuring his political convictions, which had not withstood the test of reality, he left his masters. They set Italian terrorists on his heels, who sadistically murdered one of his girlfriends and pursued him across France.

"In fact," asked Terrier at this point in their reading, "what really happened?"

"In general, that's what happened," said Blue Suit. "Only the details were a little more complicated. Cox gave you up to Rossana Rossi. But he didn't want you to get killed; he merely wanted to make trouble for you, to make you come back. So you had to be put on your guard. He had your apartment ransacked, he had you threatened on the phone, and he put an inept tail on you. He finally gave you up to Rossana Rossi, but only after your departure from Paris."

"Who massacred Alexa Métayer and my cat?" asked Terrier.

"Cox always maintained that it was the Rossi group. That's likely, because it was Rossana who left the dead cat at your hotel. Anyway, the details are no longer important. Right?"

"Right," said Terrier. "Right. They're no longer important."

At the end of the book, the narrator went back to work to

attack Sheikh Hakim, whom the PLO wanted eliminated. But he sabotaged the assassination attempt with the help of the French DST, whom he had contacted and whose undercover agent encountered a heroic death.

"And you find all this credible?" asked Terrier.

"Of course. You can trust me on that. I've overseen several books of this kind."

Blue Suit smiled confidently. The next day, he received a message from his superiors, who forbade publication of the work on the grounds that it was perfectly ridiculous.

22

"So what does this mean: 'we're canceling everything'?" Terrier asked when Blue Suit brought him up to date. "What does this mean: 'we're dropping it'? Shit!" he yelled. "I've practically learned this damn book by heart for my testimony!"

"There won't be any testimony," said Blue Suit. His face was haggard, and his blue suit was rumpled; he had cut himself shaving. "Everything has been canceled. The operation has been terminated. You have been declared legally incompetent. On the judicial level, your case has been dismissed. It will be said that you have been committed to a psychiatric clinic in the United States. Don't interrupt me, you little shit—I've had it up to here with you!" he shouted when Terrier protested vociferously. "In fact, we're going to put you back in circulation, tucked away somewhere with a false identity. We don't want to hear any more out of you. You should be glad to be so lucky."

"Lucky?" Terrier yelped.

"You massacre three dozen people, and we're nice enough to put you back on square one!" the other man yelled. "You don't call that luck?"

"I don't know," said Terrier said slowly in an undertone.

23

Anne left him in the autumn of that year. At first, she had agreed to live with Martin Terrier, to start a new life under a new identity in a town in the French Ardennes. The fact that the man had sustained a passion for her for so long, combined with the violent experiences they had shared, had made a deep impression on her, or at least so we may surmise.

But she soon tired of an existence entirely lacking in adventure—not to mention money, for Martin Terrier, under his new identity and with his current abilities, could find work only in the restaurant business: he was now a waiter in a brasserie. She also grew tired of three-minute coitus, or so we may surmise. In any case, she left suddenly and without explanation. And she has not reappeared in Nauzac, although she owns property there. May we surmise that she is running around the world and leading a passionate and adventurous life? We may; it's no skin off our nose.

24

Martin Terrier had no visible reaction when he grasped that Anne had left for good (if indeed he grasped it). During the night, he had audible reactions: he moaned or maybe groaned in his sleep, making that noise that others had called blabbering and had even tried to decode.

Every now and then, these days, Terrier still blabbers in his sleep. Otherwise, as a waiter in a brasserie, he is normal. He performs his duties properly, even if he is sometimes physically clumsy. It has recently been noted that this clumsiness increases when he drinks. Late at night, young people occasionally have fun buying him drinks until he behaves in an eccentric manner. He has even climbed up on a table and bleated like a sheep, interspersing this with grand operatic arias. Each time he is brought to such extremes, he gets angry and violent immediately afterward. But he is not dangerous, for he has indeed become so very clumsy that when he tries to hit someone, he succeeds only in falling on his face.

He lives in a small apartment.

25

And sometimes this happens: it's winter, and it's dark. Coming down directly from the Arctic, a freezing wind rushes into the Irish Sea, sweeps through Liverpool, races across the Cheshire plain (where the cats lower their trembling ears as it howls and passes over); this freezing wind crosses England and the Straits of Dover; it traverses gray plains and comes knocking directly on the windowpanes of Martin Terrier's small apartment, but these windowpanes do not vibrate, and this wind has no force. On such nights, Terrier sleeps quietly. In his sleep, he has just assumed the prone firing position.

Paris, 1979–1981